From the author of The **PATERSON PIMP**
&
MY SOUL is STILL PIMPIN' (PART 2)

How She Became A HOE

RANDY JACKSON a.k.a JASHON

Randy Jackson a.k.a Jashon

Author's Note: The characters and events in this book are fictitious. Any similarity to real persons, living or dead is coincidental and not intended by the author.

Printed in the United States of America
10 9 8   7 6 5 4 3 2 1

ISBN: 978-0-578-08250-9

First paperback edition

E-mail: Jashon763@aol.com
Website: www.ThePatersonPimp.com
facebook: Randy Jashon Jackson

Other books by Randy Jackson a.k.a Jashon:

The PATERSON PIMP
MY SOUL is STILL PIMPIN'

J&M Production Publishing
52 Washington Street
P.O. Box 20
Paterson, New Jersey 07501

Cover by: Toni (tirvolino@aol.com)

This book is dedicated to my father,

Willie "Jack" Jackson
October 28, 1927—July 10, 2010

I once heard that pain was temporary and glory was forever. Well, my dad died in July, and it still hurts me every day. I would like to emphasize that he is deeply missed. Our hearts are still broken but we thank God for the fantastic years we've spent together.
Dad, you are a legendary hero,
who is gone but not forgotten.

I love you,

Randy "Jashon" Jackson
a.k.a
The Paterson Pimp

Acknowledgments

I would like to give thanks to several people:

KARLA DENISE BAKER,
Author of *Anonymous, Sleepin' Wit' the Virus &
Kreepin' Wit' the Virus*

She really came through for me in a big way. Her help on this book was outstanding. She helped me on every aspect of getting this project done. I would never be able to repay her true worth, so once again I say, thank you and I wish nothing for you, but the best success. I would also like to thank her for the foreword she put in my book.

TONI IRVOLINO,
I would like to send a big thank you out to Toni, who once again designed my book cover.

RAQUI,
I would like to thank, Raqui, who keeps my website:
www.ThePatersonPimp.com
up and running.

FOREWORD
by

BARRACUDA BYTCH

"SETTLE DOWN!"
"C'MON, NOW..."
"OKAY, OKAY."
"CAN I GET A WORD IN EDGEWISE?"
"C'MON YA'LL."
"CALM DOWN."

I know. I know what you're thinking. What happened to Randy Jackson a.k.a Jashon? Is he getting soft, all of a sudden? Well, all I can say is based on this particular book that possibly he is maturing in stages. I gotta give him props for taking a leap of faith of this magnitude and devoting time and energy to writing a book like this. Who better to do it than the man who claims the title as: *The Paterson Pimp*...

Now he's taking it to the next level with, "*How She Became A Ho*e." I think this is a powerful step in the right direction for young girls and women from all walks of life to understand how someone can subject themselves to this tainted, however, lucrative profession. Young girls and women are often judged based on how they live their lives, but what we fail to understand is that we don't know why or how this all came about. All we know is that *she* is a hoe, and that is the bottom-line.

Now, because of "*How She Became A Ho*e," we are being given an inside look at how it all began for most

5

of these girls and women. I don't think these girls or women woke up thinking, I'm going to grow up to become a hoe. I'm more than certain that they all had other aspirations but something occurred in their lives, something so unimaginable to us, but real to them. Everything of aspiration became everything of survival —a means of support, no matter how degrading it may seem to us. This is the path they chose. Why? Well, this is what you are about to find out as you read their intimate and powerful stories.

Most think, it ain't gonna happen to me. Well, it could've easily happened to me when I was eighteen years old with a ten-month old baby in my arms after my dad had kicked me out in a November '86 blizzard. I had just graduated from high school in June of that same year. I had just turned eighteen three months later, and just that instantly my life had changed. BAM! I was homeless. But I was one of the lucky ones. I had never been approached or persuaded to sell my body for monetary gain. Never. And I give it all to God, because it could've easily happened to me. I don't dismiss anything but I do know what I will allow myself to be influenced by. Everyone has a choice but sometimes our circumstances outweigh our morals and values. Trust and believe if it had happened to me I would be one of the voices in this book. **BARRACUDA BYTCH** has nothing to hide especially if it is going to make an impact in someone else's life.

—BB

Dear Jashon,

Hi. Um, my name is Alice. Just Alice or Ally is fine. And, um, (eyes looking down at me feet), um… I'm a *hoe* in the sense that I've lived the life, whether I chose to do it or was forced to do it, it really doesn't matter much. See um, I'm still trying to figure out if this will haunt me for the rest of my life. Things seem to follow you even when you are no longer doing wrong, you know. People will always remind you of your dirt especially if you got down-'n-dirty with 'em. To me, the past *is* never really "the past" because it is still a part of your life. You did it; you lived it, so rightfully so you own it. Just like anything you have to take ownership for your setbacks and shortsightedness. I think this is my first attempt.

It may sound funny or stupid but I wonder if they have Hoes Anonymous for young girls, women, or even boys and men like me. You know how people say: "once a cheat, always a cheat"—"once an addict, always an addict"—"once a player, always a player." Does that same rule apply for *hoes*? Does the stigma *ever* go away? Maybe you know the answer to that question, Jashon.

Well, you asked for a true story. Um, (deep breath, eyes welling up), this is difficult, more difficult than I *ever* anticipated. Okay, okay, sniffling, I can do…this. Yes, I can.

This story is dedicated to all the Hoes who want out. Maybe this will give you the strength that you need before it is too late.

—Alice B.

Preface

Paterson, New Jersey

I stepped out of my flowery panties and matching training bra, turned the nozzle on to the shower letting the lukewarm water steam up the sky-blue bathroom. As I looked at myself in the mirror, I was no longer the little girl named Alice Banks. Alice seemed to have vanished right before my eyes. And an exotic dancer named Desire reappeared.

Alice became the target, while Desire became the bait. Both were setup to falter, but one was determined and destined to resume her fate.

This is how the story goes of how she became a hoe.

At a very young, vulnerable age, I loved to explore my body. You know, touch myself. At first, it was while I was taking a shower. I was probably around ten going into eleven. Underdeveloped, with no pubic hairs on my vagina and flat-chested, yet I always prayed for the day when my body would fill out with curvy thickness drenched in creamy chocolate like my mom Michele.

I was a child, an innocent person, flustered. I reached for my virgin white washcloth, and then stepped into the shower allowing the water to drench my small body. I reached for the Dove soap rubbing it into a foamy lather with the washcloth, then bent over to begin from my feet working my way up to my neckline. I caressed my skin until it was covered in what looked like a million tiny white bubbles. My soft smooth hands touching myself aroused me. I loved the pleasure it gave me, especially when I'd stick my middle finger in my little hole and moved it in and out, in and out. The feeling was so addicting.

Often I wondered was it wrong to pleasure my pussy. Had I been a product of incest? I didn't know why that thought had crossed my mind, but it did. I always seemed to nix stupid thoughts out of my head because they seemed absurd. I am no different than any other ten-year-old girl, I told myself. No different, but was I?

The lathered washcloth gently rubbed against my blackberry nipples stimulated them to hardened rocks. This unfamiliar sensation throbbed between the lips of my pussy that shot up and down the crack of my small ass. It used to make me giggle inside feeling a sense of complete gratification to my ten-year-old self. This became a routine when I'd take my showers. But then suddenly the inner giggles turned to tears on the outside of me as I recalled a little less than one year later how my mother, Michele would make me take showers. Everyone knows that when you are forced to do something it takes the fun and pleasure out of it. Well, I felt the same way. This was not uncommon behavior for a mom to want her child to have good hygiene practices. But deep within me, it seemed like there were pieces missing from this puzzling childhood. I mean why was mom making my childhood a living hell? Why was I crying because of taking a shower? It didn't make much sense to me, you know. But for some odd reason the tears transformed from tears of pleasure to tears of pain. The nightmares began too. But somehow, I always seemed to keep a smile on my small face even though I felt lousy inside.

I wondered why *they* often tried everything to rob me of my innocence and youth-hood. They destroyed my childhood in ways that I never wanted to divulge to anyone, not even to my own consciousness. But there was no way to run or hide. Who did this to me? How am I still standing? Honestly, my Father in heaven had a lot to do with my growth and spirituality. Without that belief of Him, I didn't know where I'd be. I didn't. Alice could've been another statistic: inmate, drug addict, or dead. I felt like I had beaten the odds. I truly did.

I felt myself slithering back in that ten-year-old frame again. The warm water beaded down on my long jet-black hair, down my straight-framed body, and rolled in between my toes and off of my smooth-skinned feet. *I hope you two black muthafuckers rot in hell*, I thought, as my body gave way and collapsed to the floor of the bathtub. Tears poured from my almond-shaped brown eyes, while the water splashed upon my feeble body. I tell you no lie; I needed Jesus to help uplift my spirits. I needed Jesus to help me accept what had happened to me. It was difficult and I knew it would be to ever forgive my parents for what they had done to me. It was going to have to take a lot of prayer and forgiveness.

***

Everything prior to my eleventh birthday seemed to be great in my life. I had fond memories, from what I recollect. I never really knew Randy. Oh, my estranged dad. My mom worked two jobs doing what, (I'd rather not say…it wasn't anything illegal), and she went to college part-time. Around five my mother's parents were killed in a car accident. My granddad had a heart attack on the way to church and his vehicle veered into another car causing a head-on-collision with a tractor-trailer. They were killed instantly. Even at five, I knew that I would never see my grandparents again, as they were being lowered in the ground at the cemetery in Fairlawn, New Jersey. Kids know more than their parents seemed to think they do. I remember Michele telling me that my grandparents had gone to live with God in heaven. And I had asked her, "Then why are they being buried in the ground, Mommy?" I used to ask her that question all the time. Michele would reply, "Alice, first, they are buried in the ground. Then the angels come at night and carry them to heaven to live with God." I said, "Oh." But deep down I wasn't fully convinced. She lost me when she said that the angels carried them to heaven. It sounded bogus to me; at least she tried to comfort me at our time of loss. I mean she could've been a bitch about it, but she wasn't.

My grandparents left everything to Michele. With all the insurance policies and real estate Michele would inherit well over $200,000.00. My grandparent's really used their brains. They were smart people. They invested their money. They made wise choices in life. My grandfather owned a Dry Cleaner for thirty years. My grandmother had been a nurse for twenty-five years. Life had been good to them after moving from Macon, Georgia, to Paterson, New Jersey, many years ago. They were childhood sweethearts. They only had one child, Michele. And they made sure they left her to reap all the riches they had.

Michele had left home after getting pregnant with me, after refusing to get an abortion. She managed to get an apartment. She found a job and enrolled in community college. My mother had a plan to better her life. Sometime after that, I was born. When I became old enough Michele returned back to work and school. She only asked for money from her parents when she had no other options, although she kept a good, but distant relationship with them. Michele never really forgave her parents for wanting her to have an abortion. Even though deep down inside she knew that they just wanted the best for their daughter. It didn't help that Randy was twice my mother's age. Randy was a streetwise pimp and drug dealer from the school of hard knocks and the depth of the gutter. Just like mom I was brought up sheltered from many things. I attended public school, not private like my mom. I always noticed dimness in my mother's eyes every time she talked about my dad. She talked about how he was a no good dangerous man, but how well-dressed and fine of a man he was too. Sometimes I'd get confused. I mean either he was ruthless or he was fine, well dressed or ruthless. Michele would tell me that I got my good looks from my dad. His dark brown nice complexion, thick eyebrows, thin lips and deep dimples, but she'd say that I got my bedroom eyes from her. I'd only met Randy at my sixth or seventh birthday party, and just by looking at him I couldn't see the resemblance. Or maybe I didn't want to see it.

***

13

I was always the "best dressed" in my class. The other kids, mostly white looked up to me and admired me. Michele made sure I wore nothing but the best: Baby-Phat, Guess, Calvin Klein, Reebok, Nike, diamond earrings, and 14-karat gold jewelry. Every year on my birthday I had a party at home and Michele would buy pizza and cupcakes for my class. My mother was very active in the PTA meetings, back to school nights, and she even joined me on school field trips. She did it all while working and attending college. And in return, I excelled in my academics. I made the honor roll with straight A's every marking period with an occasional B, every now and then.

I used to run home to our nanny Angelita, anxiously awaiting my mother to get off of work, so that I could showoff my report card. Angelita was tall, wide-hipped, with long silky black hair. She was an average-looking woman. There was nothing that really stood out about her, except her erotic chocolate brown eyes. But she was nice and she took pride in her job. Michele was always coming home different hours. Often my mother said she'd wished she didn't have to work so hard. If only my grandparents hadn't left the money in yearly installment payments, perhaps my mother could've managed the money better.

Even though it was just Michele and I, we got along beautifully in our one family two-floor home. Even with the live-in nanny the house was still too big for us. Five bedrooms, living room, dining room, bathroom on each floor and one in the modern basement, back patio with above ground pool. We had a washer, dryer, and dishwasher. Big screen TV's in every room and a movie projector in the living room, which no one ever watched or entered. A large kitchen table that always stayed set. We were living the life. Living large, as some would say.

Two hours later, Michele entered the front door. I jumped up from the dining room floor where I was laying playing one of my new video games. "Mommy, Mommy! Look! I made the honor roll again!" I said, excitedly. Michele picked me up and began putting wet kisses all over my face and nose. She never even looked at the report card. She knew from the past that it was nothing but straight A's anyway.

Angelita greeted Michele, "Ms. Banks, dinner is ready. Should I start preparing the plates?" Michele put me down and replied, "Yes, please, I'm so hungry I could eat a horse." Michele headed toward the bathroom to wash her hands. And I was right on her heels. Angelita yelled at me, "Alice, let your mother freshen up, alone. Go use one of the other bathrooms to wash your face and hands. It's time for dinner." I dropped my head and frowned. Angelita pulled her dishtowel out of her apron and pretended to chase me throughout the house. "You bettu fux dhat face, little girl," Angelita spoke in her island accent. The frown on my face quickly turned to laughter between the two of us.

Angelita had been with us for a little over three years. We were like one big family. We loved Angelita and she loved us too. Every since my grandparents had died, Angelita had been my mother's nanny. I was almost nine years old, at that time. And I was a happy little girl.

After dinner, Michele went to sit in the dining room and fell fast asleep. She never even saw my report card. Around eight o'clock, Angelita put me in the shower and tucked me in bed. This was how many of my nights would end. Michele exhausted and knocked out and Angelita tucking me in for bed. I never really cared much as long as I got to kiss my mother good night.

My 10th birthday was approaching. Michele had gone all out to throw me a bangin' party. The entire backyard was decorated with balloons and ribbons. There was a large banner that read: HAPPY 10TH BIRTHDAY, ALICE! Michele had a clown come and do face paintings, magic tricks, and cartoon characters with the balloons. There were about 35-50 kids from my class and neighborhood who attended. The whole party had cost her a fortune, but she didn't care. She wanted to give me the best of everything.

The only thing that seemed to bother Michele was that my father, Randy couldn't or wouldn't share this time with me. He had been missing in actions since he last stopped by about three years ago, to see me for the first time. That day my mother's eyes had bloody murder embedded in them when she laid eyes on Randy. I don't know exactly what she was thinking but I'm sure it wasn't anything good. The last time we'd both seen Randy; my mother had cussed him out and threw his tired ass out of *our* house. "GET THE FUCK OUT OF MY GODDAMN HOUSE YOU NO GOOD PIMP AND DOPE DEALER! AND DON'T EVER COME BACK! WE DON'T NEED YOUR MONEY OR YOU!" Randy just bent down and hugged me as I was crying hysterically from them arguing. He kissed me on the cheek and said, "I'll always love you. And I'll be back, one day. You're daddy's little girl." My mother wasn't trying to hear that. She pointed her index finger toward the door and yelled at him one last time, "STAY OUT OF OUR LIVES, WE DON'T NEED YOU!" Randy exited out of our home and Michele slammed the door in his sorry ass face. She had had it.

Michele stared in a trance as she remembered meeting Randy on her way home from Paterson Catholic high school. It was her senior year. Randy had pulled up on her in a brand spanking new Cadillac. He looked like a celebrity with all his jewelry and diamonds on. Till this day she said she doesn't know what made her jump in his car. I mean she didn't know anything about him. He could've been a murderer or pervert for all she knew. And plus, he was an older man too.

From that day forward somehow Randy had won Michele over with gifts and great times. He spoiled her silly. Even though my mother hid the relationship from her parents, Randy and mom managed to have a great year together. More than any other senior in her high school would have dreamed of having. Randy made her feel special. She assumed she was top priority in his life. Not too long after, Michele found out that she was pregnant. She was beyond scared. How would she explain her irresponsible behavior to her parents? It wasn't easy. It became even more difficult because my mother had no idea of what Randy did for a living. He told her that he was into real estate. But truth be told, Randy was the head of a drug crew who dominated half the city. And he also was the man behind a prostitution ring that serviced white-collar workers and many important people—people with high status and deep pockets. With Michele being a couple of months shy of eighteen, Randy thought it would be best to disappear for a while. He had also tried to offer Michele money to have an abortion, but his talks fell on deaf ears. Michele was having her baby and her parents as well as Randy couldn't stop her.

On several attempts Randy tried to tell Michele some lame excuse as to why he was absent from my life. He always blamed it on his upbringing and disbelief that I was even his biological daughter. Michele could not believe that he tried to play with her emotions by having her thinking that her child, their child, wasn't his. Michele knew it was another one of his cop-outs so that he wouldn't have to be a responsible father and help take care of me, financially.

Randy was my mother's first, everything. And Randy knew that to be true. Michele was not the type of girl to go out having promiscuous sex with men. She had too much self-respect to start running rampant just giving her pussy away. My mom had class. She wasn't anybody skank.

The backyard was crowded with kids, running amuck. Kids eagerly stood in line to get their faces painted. We attentively watched the clown do magic tricks. There was never a dry moment. It couldn't have been a better sunny afternoon in July. It was a birthday to remember. I was the happiest birthday girl who'd ever lived.

***

When I first saw Steve Benjamin, it was like looking into the eyes of a sneaky cat. Those hazel eyes spoke without words. I'm pretty sure they made Michele melt like butter every time she looked in them. His hair was shiny black with natural waves. He was medium build. His clothes were no doubt custom made. They draped on his body, flawlessly. His jewelry sent off a sparkle that could blind you. Michele broke the silence with, "Excuse me, everyone, this is my friend Steve." Not only was it everyone's first time seeing him, but also my first time ever seeing him too. Steve bent down and kissed me on the forehead and said, "This must be the angel whose birthday is today." He reached behind his back and with a corny magician trick appeared a little gold box. It had been in his hand the whole time. He handed the box to me and said, "Happy Birthday, Alice!" I was too busy trying to read this stranger as I said in my small voice; "Thank you," but no one heard me. Michele yelled at me thinking that I was being impolite. "Alice, where's your manners. I taught you better than that. Tell Steve thank you." So I managed to drag the words out of my mouth again for the sake of mom. "Thank you, Mr. Benjamin." If it made mom happy it was worth it.

Once everything was settled with Steve, Michele must've felt all eyes on her man because she let it be known. Michele stood tall and strong in her Macy's designer suit, when she said, "Ok, ladies' and gents, he's just a man we can continue my daughter's birthday party now." Snickers and laughter could be heard throughout the crowd. As the party continued I kept my eyes on this sneaky cat…Steve. He was pulling the chair out for Michele, fixing her drinks; he was no doubt in my mind a ladies' man. And in return mom was lighting the butt of his cigarette, wiping his mouth after every bit of food he ate. I wanted to just gag. All that niceness was making me sick to my stomach.

I decided to walk around to see who was at the party. Over on the other end of the yard were Mrs. Johnson and Miss Wright who were all up in the Kool-Aid. They were two old floozies gossiping, as usual. "Chile, that's a pimp. I can smell a pimp a mile away." Mrs. Johnson said in her raspy voice. And of course, Miss Wright had to add her two cents in. "Yes, honey, something about him spells like trouble. Did you see those green eyes of his?" Right then another neighbor of ours named Thelma who was in her early thirties rolled her cocoa-brown eyes and blurted out, "Why don't you two old witches just be happy for Michele? The woman has been alone for so long now. Just be happy for her." Mrs. Johnson could not bite her tongue. She crossed her arms about her bosom and snapped, "Happy my black ass! That nigga a pimp or something, and I know he's definitely trouble with a capital T." Thelma shook her head from side to side and pursed her lips. "You two *old* bitches just jealous. You two just can't stand to see someone else happy, can you? That's a damn shame."

"Who you calling old bitches, you skank," Miss Wright snapped back. "Takes one to know one," Thelma shot back and then scrolled her eyes up and down both of them and walked away mumbling underneath her breath.

I walked over to the other end of the yard and I overheard two other neighbors named Jean and Barbara gossiping. "Girlllllllllllll," Jean slurred, "I would ride dat nigga's dick all night long!" Barbara jumped in while holding her cup of punch spiked with vodka that she had stashed in her bootleg Burberry handbag. "Shitttttttt, I would suck every drop of cum that nigga got in him," she shook her big tits like it was freezing cold. That's when crazy Nancy the recovering alcoholic who still drinks added her two cents in, "That nigga probably could make me sneeze, bust a nut, and fart all at the same time." They all broke out in laughter. Honestly, I didn't find anything funny. This was my mom's man they were gossiping about. All it did was make me keep my eyes and ears open when Steve came around. He was a man to watch especially when it came to matters of mom's heart.

The next morning when I woke up, I leaped out of bed and ran straight to my mother's bedroom. I loved sleeping in bed with her. But when I pushed Michele's bedroom door open, my whole body froze. There was Steve and Michele eating breakfast in bed. "Hey, Alice," said Mom with glee in her eyes, "You remember, Steve, right?" I couldn't move. "Come here, Alice. Come get in the bed." Mom said, while Steve just gaped at me with those green eyes of his. Mom moved over to make room for me in the middle of Steve and her. But I preferred to sit on the edge behind my mom. Steve and Michele looked at each other and smiled. I heard Michele whisper to Steve, "She's gonna need a little more time. We've been alone together for so long." Steve nodded his head. "Alice." Mom said. "Yes, mommy," I said, pulling on my thumb. "You want mommy to be happy, right?" I knew where she was going with this. "Yes, mommy," I said. Mommy sighed, and then smiled. "Well, Steve's gonna be staying here with us, because that's gonna make mommy happy, ok." At first, I looked at her like a foul odor had just passed my nose and landed on her upper lip. Then my hands met my mouth as if I was surprised by the news. I pointed my forefinger toward Steve and stuttered out. "He's gon-gon-gonna be living here?" Mom didn't hesitate to respond. "Yes, Alice, and stop pointing, it's rude." Finally, Steve cut in. "Listen Ally-cat, your mom and I are in love with one another.

Your mom loves you very much, so I'm going to take care of *you*...I mean the both of you. Is that okay with you?" It didn't take me long to respond back to Steve. "Alright, okay, I mean, yes, I guess, its fine." I was tongue-tied. I had to try to convince myself that this was the best mom could do. It wasn't easy because my mom deserved the best. Now I couldn't say for sure if Steve was that, but based on the look on my mom's face, possibly he was as close to perfection as mom was going to get. Well, just like that Steve became instant furniture in the house. My mom was relieved because she had been keeping Steve a secret from her friends and me for the last seven months that Steve and mom had been dating. I didn't know what the big secret was for. I mean if you like someone, you like them. I guess mom had her reasons. Knowing mom she wanted to make sure her relationship was at a certain level before she broke the news to family and friends. That I could understand, even as a child. Michele was very cautious of her heart. After my dad Randy, Michele had pretty much written men off. It was all about work, school, work, school, and of course me. And that's how I hoped it would've stayed but I kinda had my doubts.

***

For the first few months everything was fine. But then things gradually began to change. For one, Steve started using Michele's sapphire-blue Mercedes when his silver BMW was repossessed about the second month after he moved in. He would drop mom off at work and then drive me to school. Mom would wave good-bye to Steve and me with a huge smile on her face. Happiness was written all over mom's face. I know she was thrilled to finally have a man around. I loved the fact that Steve was around too. I could now have a father figure to drop me off at school like most of my friends.

As Steve would sometimes walk me to the front door of the school, he would hold my hand from time to time. Often he would stroke my hair and rub his light-skinned hand gently in an up and down motion on the side of my soft cheek. I would just sit there thinking that my "potential step-dad" was just a nice and caring man. I thought Michele had hit the jackpot with him. I found myself showing affection toward him by rubbing his hand when he laid it upon my thigh on our way to take me to school. I found myself falling for Steve, too, like he could really be my dad. Finally, mom and I would be happy. This was a dream come true.

When Steve would arrive to pick Michele up from work, just the look on her face told it all. Michele was head-over-heels for Steve. He was most definitely the love of her life, and mine.

As Michele waited for Steve to pick her up from work, she reached in her jacket pocket and pulled out her cell phone to call home to see if Angelita had picked me up from school. They had a system where Steve would take me to school and Angelita would pick me up.

"Hello?"

"Hi Angelita, is everything okay?"

"Yes, Ms. Banks, everything is fine. Alice is in the dining room doing her homework."

"Have you seen Steve?" Michele asked her.

"No, I haven't."

Michele glanced at her Movado wristwatch that Steve had given her as a "just because" gift, last month. "Oh, he's probably running late. He might be stuck in traffic or just late from looking for a job all day. Well, I'll see you shortly."

Angelita rolled her eyes and put on a fake smile. "Okay. See you when you get home. I'll keep your dinner warm."

After hanging up with my mom, Angelita spoke under her breath, looking for a job my ass. That man hasn't worked since he moved in here. Angelita thought back to the day when she went to the local grocery store, earlier in the day. And whom did she see…Steve cruising around with his buddies in Michele's Mercedes. Angelita couldn't stand Steve, but she'd never divulge that need-to-know information to my mom. My mom was fragile, and could easily be broken. Michele needed to be handled with tender loving care. This was a delicate situation to be in.

Angelita knew that Steve was no good for my mom, but how could she prove it. Angelita felt helpless, but she had no choice but to butt out of my mother's love affair. And plus, she was just the nanny, not her mother.

Sometimes while Michele was at work, Angelita would overhear Steve talking on the phone in their bedroom. Mostly all day he'd be on the phone sounding like he was conducting business. She never really knew if he was speaking to woman or man because he was always clever when he spoke. But one thing she did know was that Steve was nobodies' legitimate businessman. She didn't care about how lavishly he dressed or how good he smelled or how articulate he tried to talk. To her it was a façade. The gift of gab, clothes, shoes, and debonair Billy Dee wannabe charisma— all of it was a façade.

Angelita had even second-guessed the BMW he had, the mysterious repossession the same month he moved in. It seemed odd to her. She swore on a stack of Bibles that she saw some woman driving that same BMW with the same license plates, the other day. From day one of Steve saying that the car had gotten repossessed, Angelita never believed that the car was his from the get-go. But as long as he kept mom and me happy she would keep everything she knew buried inside of her, even though her island instincts told her differently. Angelita stayed quiet and prayed for Michele and me in her private quarters.

As the last two cars pulled out of the parking lot, Steve

pulled up in mom's Mercedes Benz. Michele was hot but she always kept how she felt to herself. I guess she didn't want to stirrup any drama between her and Steve. It seemed odd because mom was not one to bite her tongue. I guess she was trying to keep the peace even if it bothered her.

"I'm sorry, baby." Steve said, "I was all the way across town filling out applications. It won't happen again, I promise, sweetie." Steve then leaned over and kissed her on the forehead. That was all it took for Michele to say, "No problem, let's just get home. I'm hungry and I have homework to do. I have two classes tomorrow." While they were sitting in the parking lot, two of mom's coworkers, Lois and Jackie happened to be walking out. Lois was in her mid-thirties, with deep dark chocolate skin. She was short, fat, and divorced with two children and one on his way to college. Jackie was tall, lanky with light skin that was blemished, small breasts and a flat ass. She looked to be in her mid-forties. She wasn't attractive but she was nice, when she wanted to be.

Anyway, Lois and Jackie were walking toward Lois maroon Ford Taurus that was parked a space from where Steve and Michele sat. Steve's cell phone ring tone bellowed, "You know it's hard out here for a pimp..." so he stepped out of the car to take the call. Michele found it to be strange but again, she didn't say anything. As Michele was sitting on the passenger side she had her window cracked so she was able to overhear Lois and Jackie's conversation.

Lois and Jackie both shook their heads. Then Lois pursed her full, thick lips and rotated her neck with attitude, "Ain't no way in the world I'ma let my man hold my car, while I'm at work and the MF picks me up late... everyday. No way." Jackie chuckled and said, "I know Steve from my girlfriend Jane. He ain't nothin' but a smooth talking free-loading-cocaine-sniffing-two-bit-petty hustler. I heard he got plenty dick, but don't know how to use it...but his tongue will have you doing cartwheels, back flips, and speaking in tongue." They both broke out in laughter as they threw their hands up to wave; see you tomorrow, to Jackie as she started walking toward her white Honda Accord. "Love gonna get you!" Lois yelled. "Shut up, bitch." Jackie shot back. "Lois, she could've heard you, bitch." Lois sucked her teeth, frowned up her face, and shot back, "I don't give a fuck." Michele pretended not to hear them but she heard every word. She lowered her head. The driver's side door opened and Steve got back into the car, put the car in reverse, and they headed home in silence.

***

Michele became acquainted with weed and the only culprit who had introduced her to it was *Steve*. "You got anymore weed, honey?" Steve sat on the edge of their bed and slowly turned his head around and just looked at Michele sitting at her desk. "No, I don't, baby." Steve replied. Michele sighed a bit disappointed. "I need something to give me some oomph. I have to finish this project for class." Steve remained quiet and then said, "Listen, baby, I have something that will give you energy. It'll make you feel even more beautiful than you already are. It will take you where you've never been before." Michele eyes widened she was all ears. "What is it, honey?" Steve rose to his feet and walked over to the closet and pulled out a duffel bag, unzipped it, reached his hand in and pulled out a piece of aluminum foil. He walked back over to the bed and sat down. Michele rose to her feet and sat beside him with curious eyes. Steve unraveled the aluminum foil and the white powder inside sparkled. "This is cocaine, baby. Please don't jump to conclusions or judge me. I just use a little when I'm down and sell a little to keep money in my pocket." Michele's eyes beamed and she was sort of in disbelief. "Cocaine?" she said, eyes staring at it. Steve nodded his head. "Yes, this is cocaine. It's harmless, honey." Michele continued to stare at it and then she cut her eyes at the mirror against the wall. "Do I look okay, Steve?" Steve just looked at her. "Woman, you are gorgeous." Michele smiled. It was crazy how Michele, the confident woman suddenly needed validation from *Steve*. Steve stuck his pinky in the cocaine and said, "This will give you the boost you need to do whatever you want." Michele knew it was wrong but something inside of her was eager to try it even though she had heard many bad things about it. The way she felt for Steve persuaded her to trust in his word.

Steve scooped some up with the straw that was also wrapped in the aluminum foil and held it under her nose. "Sniff, baby, sniff," he told her. Michele accidentally exhaled and the powder flew in the air. Steve laughed at her. "No. Like this." he said, and then showed her how to do it. He scooped some up and held it up to his nose and inhaled. Michele took note as the powder vanished up his nostrils. "Here you go, baby. Sniff." Michele held one nostril closed and sniffed. She squinted her eyes. "One more time in the other nostril," Steve said. At first, Michele didn't feel anything but then suddenly she felt a warm feeling that started from the tip of her toes, and proceeded to her feet, and then up to her ankles. The higher the warmness would rise the better she felt. She felt light. All she could do was smile, hard. She had an outer body experience. It was like she was dangling in mid-air looking down at herself. *Damn! This is the best feeling in the world. An orgasm has nothing on this feeling*, she thought to herself.

"Michele, Michele, you okay, baby?" Steve asked her.

"Give me some more. I want to feel like this all the time," Michele said. "Slow down, little lady." Steve said, and then scooped up some more coke and let Michele hit it again. And that's how the night went for the next couple of hours. Steve was smiling on the inside and out. He knew after they finished sniffing coke he would lick and suck her into a million orgasms. And he knew as long as he kept coke in her nose and his tongue in her pussy Michele would love him for a long time.

***

"WHERE THE FUCK IS MY MONEY? WHERE THE FUCK IS MY MONEY, STEVE!" The husky voice on the other end of the phone snapped. Steve pulled his phone from his ear, and then spoke in a nervous tone. "Look, um, ah, Rayvon, I'm sorry I fucked up, but my…" Rayvon interrupted him, "But HELL! Listen, I gave you something and that something was worth $20,000.00. Nigga, now if you smoked it, sniffed it, or lost it. Look, I really don't give a fuck what you did, but I do know that you betta have my motherfucking money this week. If I don't have it by Friday you owe me $25,000.00, you got me?" Steve started stuttering. "But-but-but Ray, listen man, ah, my woman…" CLICK!

Damn, he hung up, Steve whispered to himself. His thoughts were racing in his head. He knew Michele had another couple months until she received her check. She would receive $20,000.00 every year on her birthday, for ten years, $10,000.00 for the next 5 years totaling $250,000.00 in all. Steve knew he would have to hide from Rayvon until Michele got her dough, then he could flip it or disappear until he figured out his next move. All he knew was that Big Ray was dangerous and known for hurting or even killing anybody who fucked up his money.

Steve had got himself in a situation and he knew it was not one that would go away with a blink of an eye. This was serious. Steve rubbed his crotch over and over. He licked his lips just as fast again and again. The sight he saw really had his coked-up brain excited. As he stared in the crack in the door, he wondered why he let his habit get him in trouble with Rayvon, of all people. *$20,000.00, I mean, $25,000.00 he owed this motherfucker for that kilo*, Steve thought to himself like he was in shock or something. Maybe he was because he knew if he didn't get that dough, he was done for.

It had been weeks since Rayvon gave him a deadline on the money he owed. Since then, Steve had manipulated Michele into moving to a city closer to her job. He never told her the real reason why they had to move. That $25,000.00 he owed "Rayvon" was big news in the underground world. He thought to himself, everything would be all right soon. He would convince Michele to give him the insurance money for an investment, if not all of it, at least half of it. He knew if everything went right he could turn $10,000.00 into $30,000.00 or $40,000.00 in weeks with the right connections as long as he didn't touch his product and did the right thing.

***

How am I going to slow Michele down off of this coke, Steve wondered. She was sniffing coke every day, all day. Her habit had well surpassed what Steve ever thought it would. He had broken a cardinal rule: *never turn your woman on to drugs*. Michele's appearance was starting to change. Her attitude was always erratic. She even started missing days from work and was almost ready to drop out of school. If it weren't for Angelita nothing around the house would've gotten done. Michele hardly slept anymore. Her choice of friends had changed too. It was no longer the PTA moms meeting once a week. Now she was hanging with the coke moms who met every other night to *sniff* and drink.

As Steve peeked through the crack in the door he swore he would put everything back together. All it would take was a plan, a perfect plan. As he unzipped his pants and pulled out his dick he started jerking off, he harbored the thoughts in his head of how to hoodwink Michele and Alice.

She is almost 11 now and just starting to develop. She can easily pass for 15 maybe 16, Steve thought to himself. He knew a lot of perverts from his days as a pimp. He had once had nice stable of hoes before his habit took over. He knew if he could just grind up some money while he waited for Michele to get her check he would be straight. Just before he closed his eyes to cum, he said to himself, I'm gonna get me some of that young pussy in between selling it to my pervert customers. At that very moment, he closed his eyes as cum shot from his dick like a rocket. He was jerking it, fast and vigorously. Then he let out an *mmmmmmmmmm* sound.

***

I was in the shower rubbing my lathered body down, when I felt eyes on me. Quickly I pulled the shower curtain back and saw Steve in the bathroom door. I thought I had locked the door. I knew I locked the door. Our eyes made contact as I shivered in my skin. I screamed, as Steve dashed out of the bathroom. Immediately Angelita ran to the bathroom. "What, what, what, Alice, what's the matter?" I tried to get myself together, tried to stop the shivering the best I could. "Nothing," I replied, looking down at my wet feet. "I-I-I-thought I saw something. I mean someone. I mean nothing." My voice dropped to a whisper, "Never min." Angelita just looked at me, puzzled, and asked, "Are you sure?" I kept staring at my feet and replied, "Yes, I'm sure." I didn't know why I didn't just tell her the truth. I knew that Steve was watching me take a shower. After that one intrusion I always felt Steve's eyes on me.

After a while, the thought of Steve watching me dissipated. But in the back of my mind I felt like I should share what happened with Michele. But Steve did something that brought everything to light before I got a chance to tell her myself.

Michele yelled with eyes the size of gumballs. "What are you doing, Steve?! Are you high or something?" Steve was peeking through the crack in the door as Angelita was leaving the bathroom. Steve straightened himself up and said, "No. I'm okay. I'm just getting ready to jump in the shower. Make sure you save me some blow. That's all we got until tomorrow." Michele heard him but it flew right over her head as she walked back into their bedroom, sat down, and scooped up a nice amount of coke with a matchbook and then took two more big hits before laying back and drifting in ecstasy.

Mr. Palmer cleared his throat and took another sip of his coffee as Michele walked in with her union delegate, a solid framed woman named Mrs. Williams. Glenda, well, Mrs. Williams was tall, caramel complexioned, with short auburn hair and big mahogany eyes. "Please ladies have a seat." Mr. Palmer said and then leaned back in his burnt-rust executive chair. They both sat down and stared into his ivory-colored face. Mr. Palmer looked to be in his early fifties. He looked at Michele with his bright blue eyes and cut to the chase in his professional voice. "Ms. Banks, your random drug test came back positive for cocaine and the… Now let me just say we love you very much here at Masons. You have worked hard and given us many great years of dedicated service. We would love to have you work here many more years, but you'll have to complete a 30 day inpatient or a 60 day outpatient program." Michele leaned over to her delegate and whispered in her ear. Mrs. Williams spoke in a delicate tone. "Mr. Palmer, we would like another test taken because it has been a known fact that specimens can be lost, tampered with, or how easy an mistake can be made. We would like to know why Ms. Banks was randomly tested in the first place and who ordered it. According to the rule book it states that an employee must show signs of strange behavior for a random test to be ordered." Mr. Palmer and Mrs. Williams went back and forth with the rules and regulations, all Michele was thinking about was getting another hit of coke and her insurance check that was coming in a couple of weeks.

***

"TWO THOUSAND!!" Steve yelled into the phone. Listen…she *is* a 16 year old virgin." The soft-spoken businessman replied, "Look Steve, the agreement was for one thousand dollars. And how do I even know that this young lady is a virgin." Steve was trying to keep his cool but it wasn't easy. He was desperate, and desperation could fuck any deal up. Steve massaged his chin trying to think of a way to assure his client that he was a man of his word. "Listen Mr. Dempsey, it was a thousand dollars until I found out that she was for *you* and *your* wife. It's a thousand a piece." Mr. Dempsey repeated himself. "And how do I know that she is a *virgin*?" Steve assured him again. "I know she is, trust me." Mr. Dempsey paused, while Steve was sweating bullets. "Ok, I'll give you fifteen hundred for two hours." Mr. Dempsey said. Steve vigorously shook his head on the other end of the phone. "Fifteen hundred will only get you an hour and a half. Two thousand will get you two hours." They both paused. "You drive a hard bargain, Steve. You got yourself a deal. Two hours for two thousand. See you at 8 o'clock tonight." Mr. Dempsey said. Steve grinned from ear to ear.

"See you at 8:00 p.m." They both hung up the phone. With the thought of receiving two thousand dollars, Steve was ready to put the second part of his plan into effect. *If Michele doesn't agree to let me take Alice, then I'll take her by force,* He thought to himself. Shit, he said to himself, I would kill my momma for two thousand right now. Just cold kill her without as much as shedding one tear.

***

Michele walked out of the building fuming mad. Steve was in the parking lot waiting. She jumped in the car cursing up a storm. She went on and on about how she had dedicated her whole life to this company and how she felt wronged by them. First, she felt wronged by them for giving her a drug test. And secondly, by how they wanted her to go to a program even though she knew she had a drug problem. She was by no means giving up her cocaine at this stage in the game. She was yelling louder in the car. Steve's mind was on his own agenda. The only thing I need is some money to hold me down until I get my check. Fuck this job! Michele screamed. Steve knew that this was the perfect time to step in with his plan. "Michele, baby," he said softly, "I have, I mean, we have an opportunity of a lifetime. We can make two thousand dollars. God knows we need it especially with your job situation. But I need to take Alice with me to pull it off. It's easy trust me, if I have a little girl with me the plan will come off smoothly. Two thousand dollars for nothing trust me. I would cut off my right arm before I let any danger come to you or little Alice." Michele chest heaved up and down. "Well, what is it Steve?" Steve sighed, inwardly. "Listen baby, the less you know, the better." Michle remained silent, still hot under the collar.

***

Michele knocked on my bedroom door and told me to get dressed. "Where are we going, Mommy?" I asked her. "We aren't going anywhere, you're going with Steve. Be on your best behavior, Alice," she said with a hint of attitude. I noticed that my mother was on edge about something. Possibly she and Steve were having problems. Maybe they were on the verge of breaking up. I could only hope so. It was bad enough that I no longer had Angelita to talk to. It seemed she'd been let go a couple of day's prior because *they* claimed that they couldn't afford her any longer. What changed all of a sudden? I wondered, because things looked the same around the house, except for, Michele and Steve. Their drug habit got in the way of their finances and as a result Angelita lost her job and I no longer had a mother.

It was so heartbreaking the day Angelita had to go. We hugged each other tightly and cried so emotionally, for what seemed like hours. Michele had to pry us apart. Angelita reached for her luggage and said that she was going back to her country in Jamaica. Steve wasn't even kind enough to offer to drive her to the airport. He said something about not having enough gas in the car. I was mostly surprised by my mother's actions. She didn't even bother to give Angelita a hug. She didn't even shed one tear. Not one. How cold could one be? The taxi honked its horn and Angelita took one last look at my mother and me and exited out the door. God, they treated her like crap, after all those years Angelita had worked for us. My grandparents must've turned over in their graves.

Angelita was kind enough to leave me her number, just incase I ever wanted to talk or if I ever needed her. She promised to stay in touch with me. It was difficult seeing her leave; I mean she'd been a live-in since I was five. So here I was now eleven and all by my lonesome.

Angelita knew all along that Steve was the problem in our household. He had come and destroyed what was once a happy family. My eyes welled up as I thought about how Steve and Michele stayed locked up in their bedroom like prisoners getting high, on all days, my birthday. Michele used to go all out on my birthday before Steve arrived.

Knock. Knock.

I flinched in my skin when I heard the knock at my bedroom door. "Yes." I said. "Hurry up, we are about to leave." Steve said. "Ok." I said, fidgeting as I hurried to get dressed in a T-shirt and faded Old Navy jeans and my black and hot pink Pastry sneakers.

Steve tossed Michele some more coke and said. "I'm about to leave. I'll be back in about two hours or so." He moved in to kiss her on her forehead, but he mistakenly kissed her on top of her head because Michele was moving so fast to pickup the coke. "Take care of my baby, nigga." Michele said with her eyes glued to the foil. She ripped the foil open and scooped up some and sniffed, as Steve exited out of the bedroom door.

Steve knocked on my bedroom door and yelled. "Alice, c'mon, you're going to make us late."

I opened the door and eased out with queasiness in my stomach. Suddenly I felt sick. I had this eerie feeling that something bad was going to happen to me.

The ride seemed endless to me. I mean it was just stretched road on smooth asphalt up Route 17 North heading toward Allendale, New Jersey. My eyes were growing heavy and I must've dozed off. The last thing I remember was that we rode in inaudible silence. Steve wouldn't even turn the radio on. He didn't utter one word since we left home. It really made me feel invisible.

When I awoke I had no idea of where we were. The

area was well kempt. Nice lawns that stretched for miles, it seemed. They were big houses that looked like friggin' mansions secured by tall iron gates. Immaculate parks and shopping centers that looked spanking new. The trees were tall and there were expensive cars in almost every driveway. People dressed in well-to-do clothes. I didn't see one piece of litter on the ground. Even the dogs that I saw were clean and on leashes. They looked like they hadn't missed a meal.

As the evening approached I could still see that this place was different from any place I had been. It was like country living. It smelled like it too. I even smelled horse manure lingering in the air. All the houses had fancy mailboxes that were extended toward the streets. I kinda chuckled inside, wondering why their mailboxes weren't attached to their homes like ours was at my house.

Steve turned into this spacious driveway and etched on a copper sign that was stuck to the cobblestone wall was the name: DEMPSEY. Steve approached the gate and honked the horn, twice. The gates opened backwards. From the time that we left home Steve and I hadn't spoken. But I needed to know where we were so I asked in my small voice, "Steve, where are we going?" Finally, Steve answered looking toward the road, not at me. "Well, your mom and I are having some problems…money problems…" as the car came to a stop in the back of several other cars, Steve continued, "Now these people are friends of mine, nice people. And your mother and I need you to do what they say. I want you to be nice to them." As we got out of the car I felt that same queasiness in my stomach that I had felt at home. My eyes cut over and up Steve's tall body. "Nice, how?" Steve remained silent, at this point.

We stood in front of this huge front door that had beautiful stained glass like in a church and on the welcome mat it read: Welcome to the Dempsey Home. Steve rung the doorbell and a minute later a large obese white man and a petite-sized white woman opened the door. They both had warm smiles on their faces. The man had a cup in his hand and the lady was smoking a cigarette. My body began to tremble with fear and suspension by the way they were both looking at me. It was like they were grisly monsters eating me up with their eyes. It was pretty spooky.

Steve winked his eye at the couple, which I found to be a bit strange. Mrs. Dempsey walked up to me and put her meaty arm around me and invited us inside as she walked me into the dining room. They had a beautiful home with nice and fancy stuff. Stuff that I knew cost a lot of money. She offered me to have a seat, asked if I would like anything to drink or eat. I kindly said no, thank you. Steve and Mr. Dempsey walked in the opposite direction toward what looked like a study. "What's your name, my dear?" Mrs. Dempsey asked me. "Alice," I said with my eyes wandering about the ceiling. "What a lovely name," she said, "My name is Evelyn. Call me Evelyn for now on, okay." I nodded my head up and down. "Do you like pets?" I shook my head no. "Do you dance?" I shook my head no. In the meantime, Mr. Dempsey and Steve continued to small talk. I glanced over to the room where they were and I saw Mr. Dempsey hand Steve an orange envelope. I couldn't hear what they were talking about, and as much as I tried to read their lips nothing was making sense to me.

"Are you, okay?" Mr. Dempsey asked Steve.

Steve was sweating profusely and shaking like a leaf, while clenching the envelope like it was a winning lottery ticket. "Yeah...I'm cool," Steve replied. "She looks awfully young, Steve," Mr. Dempsey said, while scrolling his eyes up and down my small body. Steve grimaced. "Ain't that how you fuckin' like 'em," Steve replied, "See you in two hours, Jack," he said, as he headed towards the door and exited out. I was ready to open my mouth to say, "Steve wait..." but the words never exited out of my mouth. That queasy feeling crept back in my stomach, though. I knew, I just knew, something bad was about to happen to me. I just knew. Whatever was in that envelope was far more important to Steve than me. Steve left me in the hands of Evelyn and Jack. I wasn't sure why. But I was soon about to find out.

Mr. Dempsey returned to the dining room and poured himself a drink of Johnnie Walker Blue. He turned the glass up and downed it in one shot. He walked over to where Evelyn and I were sitting trying to make small talk. I guess to make me feel comfortable, but it didn't work. I was on pins and needles. I kept cutting my eyes over my shoulders, wondering where Steve had gone. The palms of my hands were sweaty. Evelyn had asked if I wanted her to take my coat off when Jack pushed his wife out of the way.

"What are you doing?" Jacked snapped, "I paid two thousand dollars for *this*." Suddenly I was a "this" not a person. Jack drew his right arm back and with the force of a drunken man he swung, hard. The force knocked me back off of the couch. I began to scream for my mother and Steve to come rescue me. But my screams had gone unheard. Jack pointed his index finger on my little nose and ordered me to remove my clothes. Before I could respond or react, *WHAM*, he hit me again with a closed iron fist. Evelyn rushed over to my aid, or so I thought, but all she was trying to do was help me remove my clothes, not stop her husband. I could see fear in her eyes as she witnessed her husband using violent tactics on me, oddly enough something changed in her eyes, suddenly she was turned on. I could tell by the way she was looking at him, look at me. It turned her on so much that I could see that her nipples were hard through her winter-white turtleneck sweater. After Evelyn helped me remove my clothes, Jack picked me up and carried me to his bedroom. Their room looked like something out of Trump Hotel in New York City. As I was admiring their extravagant bedroom, Jack plopped me on their bed. All the while Evelyn kept saying, "Me, first, honey. Me, first…please, honey, me, first," as she gawked at me like a fresh piece of meat.

Evelyn undressed quickly out of her turtleneck and black slacks. She stood before me in a matching peach thong with lace bra. Her body was pale-skinned with blotches of brown patches on her skin. Her breasts were probably a 36 D cup, no stomach, and I could tell that she frequently got bikini waxes because her skin looked smooth as silk around the edges of her thong. She wasn't a fashion model, by far, but she wasn't bad on the eyes either. While Jack was undressing, Evelyn took it upon herself to sensually walk over to the bed and leaned down to kiss me on my forehead, earlobe, cheek, nose, then lips, very gently. Then she eased her wet tongue down to my little breasts covering the nipple with her warm saliva until it was saturated. She slithered her tongue over to the other nipple and did the same thing. At first, I had no reaction to her. I was shivering in my skin. But the more she did it, gently, down to my small navel; I felt something that I can't really explain come over me. I felt as if she was nurturing my innocence in a perverted sort of way, if that makes any sense. Jack, on the other hand, was not as subtle as his wife. He stood over us both, ordered his wife to get on the bed and spread them on all fours, while he jerked his penis like a mad man. He was grunting each stroke, and then he ordered Evelyn to lay me down and spread my legs as she crawled in between them. "Eat it! Eat that virgin's cunt, dear. Eat it nicccceeee and slowwww. I want us to get our monies worth." He smirked with this crazed look in his blue eyes. Evelyn eyes beamed with delight and seductiveness as she pried the folds to my lips apart. She licked the small clit very gently. I felt my body jolt. I had never felt that feeling before. A feeling that I could not explain had me stiff. "Relax, Alice, I won't hurt you," Evelyn said as she did it again. And again, my body stiffened. "Pretend that we are somewhere pleasant," she said in her soft motherly tone. I tried to do as I was told. Somewhere pleasant, I spoke in my head. I swear I couldn't think of one place. I mean it was an awkward situation. Nothing pleasant was coming through.

Evelyn stroked her tongue softly against my chocolate meat. But still, I had no immediate reaction. It felt good against my skin, but that was it. She was persistent in her quest to get off, as Jack continued to jerk his penis. The head of his penis was the shape of a dark purple plum, and the long stem was wide and thick like a large cucumber. It literally scared me to even look at it. Evelyn eased her hands up to my breasts and pulled on my tiny, hard nipples, while gently licking my clitoris. Jack walked closer to the edge of the bed and stuck one of his fingers in her moist hole. Evelyn moaned as she was licking the edges of my vagina, while Jack was still beating his dick, with those baby blues glued to me. I knew something bad was about to happen. I just knew.

Jack moved in closer to his wife and stuck his penis in her, while he eyes gazed at me. Evelyn's body began to shake as she uttered, "oh, shit, Jacccccccccckkkkkkkk, I'm cummin'!!!" She was breathing heavy, panting, trying to catch her breath. I was afraid for her. I thought she was dying or something. Then Jack turned his focus off of her and on to me. I couldn't stop shivering I was that scared.

Tears were already crawling down my face. I lay there like a prisoner. I was helpless and hopeless, as Jack pushed his wife out of the way. He jumped on top of me and forced his penis into my locked hole. Each stroke felt like he was breaking the skin. I was so tight. He knew, that I was a virgin and that only intensified his strokes. He was beckon to get inside of my domain, not concerned about how bad it hurt me. I screamed by the feel of his large penis trying to open me up. God, it felt like nothing I wanted to ever feel again. He squeezed my wrists pinning me down on the bed as he stroked, trying with all of his might to break me in. Finally, I felt myself open up, and so did he. He was breathing heavy in my ears, the smell of Johnnie Walker Blue swept across my nose. I tried turning my head from side to side but he ordered me to be still. So I did as I was told.

Forcefully Jack rammed his penis inside of me, with his left hand he wrapped it around my throat to cut off the sound of me screaming for my mother. The closer he came to reaching his climax, the more he choked me. He choked me so hard I nearly passed out. After he grunted out, "I'm cummin' you lil' bitch," he rolled his obese body over, steady spewing out profanity. Then he scrolled his eyes down and gaped at his penis seeing blood. He might've thought that I started my period, Evelyn assured him in a giggling manner, "Honey, she's a virgin, you broke her in, what do you expect." How could they be laughing at my expense, I wondered?

Owowwwwwwwwwwwwwww, I bit down on my bottom lip in excruciating pain when I awoke. My small, thin arms wrapped around my knees, tightly hugging them, as I shivered in my skin. My vagina and rectum reminded me of what had happened. God, the pain was so severe I thought, no, I wanted to just lie there and die. I felt like I was lying in a pool of my own muddy-water blood. My whole body was motionless, and in disbelief.

The chimed doorbell rang.

I could only assume that it might've been Steve. A few minutes later, the door opened to the Dempsey's bedroom and Jack ordered me to get dressed. I wasn't even allowed to freshen up. I felt dirty, nasty, and disgusting. I felt ashamed, humiliated, degraded, and distraught. I felt broken. Dismantled and unloved. I felt so many different emotions that made me feel very low about myself. Even still, I got dressed and headed toward the door, but before I exited I turned around and stared at the bed. The bed that stole my most precious jewel I swore that I'd never forget and I didn't. I couldn't. It was now a part of my makeup. And as far as I was concerned my makeup was tainted and ugly. I was damaged goods.

I guess I was taking too long and Jack came back, but this time he manhandled me and literally dragged me out of his bedroom. I kicked and screamed until he looked at me with evilness in his eyes. It was the scariest look I had ever seen in my life. By the time we had gotten down to the dining room, Steve was standing there with an expressionless look upon his face. I hated Steve. I hated him even more for leaving me with those two monsters. *How could he do this to me*, I thought.

"So, Mr. Dempsey, how did things go," Steve asked as if he was a doctor checking me out for the common cold or something. How things went, I retorted in my head. *Things went bad, realll bad*. That was a dead giveaway that Steve was behind this all along. I was eleven, not twenty. God, I hated me some *Steve*, and now *Jack* and *Evelyn* too.

Jack practically pushed Steve and me out of his door. Steve looked baffled. Before the door slammed in our faces, Jack's last words were, "I'll call you in two weeks." Steve was high on cocaine he didn't even realize the condition I was in. I was walking with my legs clamped together, moaning and groaning like I was about to die and this cokehead didn't even notice.

Steve drove without saying one word to me, as I lay silent in the backseat with tears in my eyes. Once we got close to home, he stopped at some abandoned building and demanded that I stay in the car. I didn't know what he was doing in there. I lifted my head up and I didn't see a soul outside. It was an old building that looked like it was about to fall any minute. I wished it did and killed Steve. I lay my head back down and whimpered to myself. Finally, Steve returned to the car with a package in his hand, his eyes looked glossy and red. Still, he never uttered one word to me. He turned the radio up loud and sped off. Almost every pothole in the street he hit, I felt this insufferable pain throughout my body. All I wondered was if my mom was home and if she was in on what Steve let happen to me. I felt so mistreated, so invisible, and so insignificant.

Once we arrived home, Steve exited out of the car in a rush; I slowly eased myself out of the backseat. I was walking like a snail, wincing, and whining to myself. God, it hurt to breathe. Yes, breathe.

Steve was already in their bedroom when I got to my bedroom. I didn't go into my bedroom right away, though, I eavesdropped by their door. I heard Steve talking to himself about cooking. I didn't know if he was talking about cooking dinner or what. Come to find out, Steve was truly a cokehead. He was freebasing behind Michele's back. I think apart of me wanted to believe that my mom wasn't a coke fiend. Yeah, a small part of me wanted to believe that. But as much as I wanted to believe didn't change my reality.

Steve was high as a kite. He entered their master bathroom only to find my mother laying face down on the floor. Steve thought that she had ODed. I turned the knob to their bedroom door with one of my hands between my legs trying to stop the bleeding from my vagina, as I tiptoed inside. All I remember seeing were my mother's legs sprawled on the tile floor with only her panties and bra on, and Steve standing over her. "Michele, Michele," Steve yelled above her. Michele with a head full of coke was barely able to raise her head off the floor. She answered him in a druggy voice, "What do you want man?" Steve shook his head as if he was appalled with her. "Your daughter needs you. She's in her bedroom lying on her floor bleeding and crying." Michele didn't budge, not at first, but then she said, "Nigga, help me up so that I can go see my baby." Steve leaned over and picked her up like she was lightweight. He turned the faucet on and splashed her face with cold water trying to wake her up. Michele was groggy and disoriented. In other words, Michele was high as a kite too. Looking back, I realized that those two really belonged together. They really did.

I tiptoed out of their bedroom, and quickly opened the door to my bedroom. I lay on the floor in a fetal position hopeful that my mother would come to my aid and rescue me. I moaned, "Mommy, mommy, mommy," hoping she'd feel empathy for me. In the doorway of my bedroom I saw Michele standing there, wide-eyed. She never extended out open arms to me. She never came to my rescue as I had hoped. She merely stood there gawking at me like I was some stray cat. Then she walked right passed me and opened my dresser drawer. I began to cry, loudly, needing her to comfort me in my time of need. Still, her arms never reached out for me. She snatched a pair of my flowery panties from the drawer, "Alice, it's *just* your period, damn!" She snapped at me, and then stormed out of my bedroom, then within what seemed like two seconds she stormed back in and tossed what looked like a Maxi pad on the floor like I was a dog telling me to fetch the bone that she had just thrown. "Use that to soak up the blood," she said and walked out of my bedroom without as if a care in the world. I could not tell you how that made me feels. I was eleven, eleven, broken, and now dismissed by my own mother.

I lay on the floor bawling like a little baby. I felt like Michele had stabbed me in the back with a pitchfork. Her unemotional behavior was ice cold. I cried and cried and cried. My eyes grew heavy, they were already swollen, but I kept fighting to keep them open. Just before I dozed off, I prayed to God to help my mother and me. "Please God," I said in a raspy tone, "Please, help Mommy and take Steve away from us. Please, God, please…Amen."

The next week I barely spoke to anyone. I kind of hibernated in my room as well as within myself. Most of the days and nights I cried because I felt myself falling to pieces. The worst part of this was that I no longer had my mother to talk to. Nor did I have my father. All I had was God and often I wondered if even He was listening to my outcries. Why did He allow this to happen to me? I asked myself thousand and one times.

It was three nights after the rape. Night after night I thought about the *rape*—the look on Jack's face as he was humping and pumping me. I could still smell the alcohol on *his* breath. I remember the look on Evelyn's face too as she was licking me down below. I remember that I was sprawled across my bed in my hot pink boy shorts on and mint-green T-shirt in deep thought, when Steve barged into my bedroom without knocking. I flinched, and slowly sat up, with my eyes piercing his. My heart was racing in my chest as my eyes scrolled his camel-colored Timberland boots, shaggy True Religion jeans, and wife beater T with a tattoo of a butt naked woman bowing down to a man sitting on a throne on his left shoulder. My heart was pounding loudly. God, I thought he could hear the beats. I kept trying to tell myself to relax, to be cool, to not show fear, but I know he sniffed it. He smelled the fear oozing from my pores. He had this strange look in his eyes, one that reminded me of Jack, and then without as much as a warning, he pushed me back onto my bed, pulled down my boy shorts, ripped off my T-shirt, and stood over me before crawling on the bed and repeatedly raping me for most of the night. I couldn't scream or holler. I was numb—completely frozen. I cannot remember where Michele was. I don't know if she was in their bedroom, living room, dining room, I can't remember, anything other than Steve's heavy breathing brushing against my shuddering body as he was poking his hard penis in and out of me.

***

It was nearly two weeks and the two thousand that Steve had was gone. Steve sat on the edge of the bed thinking. He knew of this perverted drug-dealer named Big Fat. Big Fat had to weigh at least three hundred pounds. He was deep dark-skinned with dreadlocks that fell past his butt. His potbelly was so big it swallowed up his belt. Every time he'd bend over he'd moon you with the crack of his ass. He was real nasty. Steve heard through the grapevine that Big Fat had a thing for watching young girls dance naked, while he shot up heroin. It was about noon when Steve gave Big Fat a ring. Steve conjured up a scheme to get Big Fat to give him some drugs and money. The tradeoff would be me. Big Fat was depending on Steve to make it happen. Steve knew all he had to do was convince Michele to let him take me in exchange for the drugs and money. Michele was so far gone she'd agree to just about anything. It only took ten minutes for Michele to be sold on the idea. Yep. Ten minutes for my mother to sell me to those monsters to feed her drug habit.

"Mommy's sick, baby. I need you to help me," Michele said, while her thin body was sprawled across her bed. "You know I love you, right? Everything's gonna be like it used to be, Alice. Real soon, okay." My mother started crying and pleading all in one breath with me. I just stood there staring at her. She looked different. I mean she had lost weight, her skin looked uneven toned. To the naked eyes Michele looked sick like she needed to go to the hospital or something. I tried to be helpful by whisperings, "Okay, mommy." I had watery eyes and all. God, I felt so bad for her. I guess because I couldn't do anything to make her feel better. Michele raised her head off of the pillow. I moved in closer to her. Our faces met as she pecked me on the cheek with wet kisses and then all over my face, "Thank you, baby, thank you, mommy loves you." I wanted to believe that she still had love for me but truthfully her actions of neglect showed me differently. Didn't she realize that I needed her? I felt abandoned. She was treating me no differently than Randy, but with Steve in her life, she couldn't see the reality of her pain or mine. She couldn't see who she had become. I suffered. Frequently I cried behind closed doors because I felt so alone, and lonely. I was eleven years old and a nervous wreck. And the sad part of all of this was that Angelita was nowhere around. This was the time when I needed her the most.

***

One day, I was in the shower. I heard the door open. Did I forget to lock it, I asked myself. Steve yelled for me to hurry up, as he stood gaping at my little body all covered in white lather. After about a minute or so he closed the bathroom door. Tears rushed down my face, I started shaking uncontrollably, while I rinsed my body down. I stepped out of the shower, and towel dried as the tears continued to fall from my eyes. All I could think about was if Steve was standing on the other side of that door. And the thought of if he was really terrified me. It literally took me about ten minutes to open the door. I was still shaking. I took one deep breath and prayed that Steve was nowhere around. I kept seeing these flashes of him on top of me, poking me hard with his large penis. I wanted to vomit, but I didn't. I wanted to scream, but I didn't. I wanted to runaway, but I didn't. I didn't do anything but go into my room, lock the door, and sit on the edge of my bed in deep thought.

As I was sitting there, I could vividly hear Steve and Michele arguing from the kitchen. There were other voices that jumped in that sounded distinctly like this guy that lived upstairs. Oh, yeah, that's right I forgot to mention that Michele had rented out her attic to this guy named Man. If I'm not mistaken, I think Steve convinced her of that to bring in some extra money to support their habit. I was often leery of Man because he always stared me up and down like he was sexing me with his eyes. He seemed like the pervert type. Uh-huh.

One day Man, the short, rotund dark-skinned man with receding hairline had offered me some money to go get me some candy. I ran like the wind from him. Now, here Man was in our kitchen. I'd always remember his dry, raspy voice anywhere.

Still sitting on the edge of the bed, there was a gentle knock on my door.

"Who is it?" I asked tucking my towel in so that it wouldn't fall exposing my small breasts.

Randy Jackson a.k.a Jashon

"Alice, it's me, mommy."

Michele walked in, sat down and placed her scrawny arm around me and gave me a big bear squeeze. "I need you to do something for my, Ally." She said in a small voice. I knew it wasn't anything good because, for one, she rarely called me Ally. Michele had this look in her eyes that I had never seen before. She was fidgety too. "You all right, mommy?" I asked her. "Yeah, baby, I'm fine, just fine." She assured me. I knew she wasn't. Her body language spoke louder than her words. She scratched her throat a couple of times, then said, "Come with me in the kitchen." I felt that sick feeling in my stomach again. "Okay, let me get dressed, first." I said. "No, no, baby, we are all family here. You don't have to get dressed. C'mon, it will only take a minute." Just hearing the sound in Michele's voice, a sound that reassured me that I would be okay, was the only reason why I believed her. We headed down to the kitchen and sitting at the kitchen table was Big Fat, Steve and Man. I looked at Michele with watery eyes. How could she hoodwink me like that, I wondered? As I tried to turn to head back to my bedroom, Michele gently grabbed my forearm before I could get away. She raised her left hand and stroked my face as she had done when I was a little girl, sick with a cold. God, I missed her touch. She looked me dead in my eyes and asked with this innocence in her voice, "Alice, all you have to do is do a little dance on the kitchen table. That's all." She stroked my face again as tears leaked from my eyes. "Baby, just close your eyes and pretend you're in your mirror dancing." I shook my head from side to side, "No, no, I don't want to. No, mommy." I replied in a crackling voice. "Shhhh. Listen, honey, mommy is sick and I need *you* to do this for me. Please, baby, please? I promise it'll be over quickly. Just, just five minutes for mommy, okay, baby, please?" I swallowed the lump that was stuck in my throat. I closed my eyes as Michele had advised and all I saw was *Jack*, *Evelyn*, and *Steve*. I gritted and grinded down on my teeth, as tears continued to pour from my weary eyes. I couldn't stand to look at Michele anymore.

I didn't know, and didn't like.

It was like I had an outer body experience or something. Steve stood and walked over to the portable CD player that was on the counter next to the microwave and slipped in a CD, while Michele was trying to convince me to let my towel fall to the floor. Man was sitting at the table with his lustful dark eyes on me. Man stood to his feet and extended out his massive hand to help me stand on top of the kitchen table. I raised my right leg, and then my left to stand on top of one of the kitchen chairs. I stood there frozen while their eight eyes were gawking at me. Michele stood on top of the chair too to help me unloosen the towel. Tears were streaming down my face like a rainstorm. I was so scared. My eyes met Big Fat and Man's and I could see them licking their full-lips at me. Big Fat's left hand was under the table rubbing his dick inside of his pants. "Okay." Steve said, "Money and the drugs, first. Tell her to dance, first. Take that towel off, Alice." He demanded. I wrapped my hands around my body trying to shield myself. But then, something deep inside of me gave in. I dropped the towel to my feet, and just stood there, naked and all. My head was lowered as if I was embarrassed. I felt myself fading, but then I snapped back to reality when I heard Steve bellow, "Dance, girl, dance!" The sound of his voice shook my bones. I heard "Sexy Motherfucker," by Prince playing in the background. I was trying to get into the music, trying to block them out of my sight and mind. I felt myself twirling my body around like I was dancing in my bedroom. The table began to shake from Man jerking himself, harder and harder. Big Fat's eyes were engrossed on me too. I could see that he had a hard-on too. He kept wetting his lips like LL Cool J. Michele cut her eyes from side to side like she was ashamed of ever letting me showcase myself in such a disgraceful fashion, but not once did she demand for me to stop. No, she merely turned away as if she had never faced eyes on me before. I became a total stranger to her. I can't tell you how much that hurt me.

At that moment I *despised* my own mother. I *hated* her with a passion. Just the look in my eyes told it all—I literally changed inside and out.

I witnessed the exchange of coke and money being handed to Steve from Big Fat and Man. Tears rolled down my face. Snot drooled down my nose. Steve no longer had any cares about me watching them get high, while I was still dancing my soul away. They started cooking the drugs. Michele and Steve were in a hurry to get high. In between that Michele kept saying, "Do it, baby. You doin' realllll good, baby," as her body started jerking to the music. Steve eased himself away from the table once he knew my mother was floating. He slipped in their master bathroom and smoked his coke through a pipe. Michele was none the wiser that Steve was freebasing, at least, not right away.

After about twenty minutes, I was getting restless. Big Fat had both of his hands under the table by now. He was jerking his dick even harder and faster as he stared at me. His black and pink lips were moving but no words were coming out. After about ten minutes, Big Fat let out a loud sound, "Ohhhhhhhhhhh, shit!" That was all you heard after he climaxed all over his hands and inside of his pants. At that moment, he closed his eyes. His head fell to the side ad he started snoring loud as hell. I jumped off the table and ran as fast as my legs could into my bedroom, slammed the door, locked it, and fell to the side of my bed and sobbed so uncontrollably to myself. I cried until I fell asleep on my bedroom floor. I swear I wanted it to be a dream. I didn't want it to be real, but I knew in my heart that it was.

***

On the other side of town, Big Rayvon sat on his white velour couch with a glass of orange juice in his hand. Steve had not yet reached out to him in months. None of Big Ray's crew had seen Steve either. With murder in his eyes and anger in his voice, Ray spoke to his crew. "That motherfucker owes me $25,000.00," he said, "I want him dead! You hear me, DEAD! And I want his bitch dead too! Them motherfuckers stole from *me*. They stole from me and nobody steals from me. I want the word out on the streets if anybody helps me find them two motherfuckers they'll get $5,000.00. Find them and kill them. It won't be too hard to find two junkies." One of Big Ray's crewmember's named Sincere raised his caramel-colored hand. "What, Sincere," Big Ray said. Sincere stood tall in his lanky frame. He had a gap in-between his two front teeth and he looked to be in his early twenties. His cornrows were neat lying perfectly against his scalp. He was an immaculate dresser and always wearing the latest sneakers. "I heard that junkie motherfucker bitch has a daughter about, oh, maybe twelve years old. What should we do if she's there when it goes down?" Big Ray pressed his hands against his mouth, pondering. Then he points his index finger at Sincere. "Listen," Big Ray, says in a smooth tone as he nods his head up and down, and then his voice roared loudly, "I DON'T GIVE A FUCK IF HIS MOTHER AND JESUS IS THERE! Kill everybody in sight. It's time I sent a message to the streets. If you fuck with Big Ray or anybody in his crew your mother better go shopping for a black dress, because you're dead, dead, motherfucking DEAD!" Right then, Big Ray drained down his glass of orange juice and waved his hand for his crew of thirteen, to leave.

As Big Ray's crew walked out the door, there was silence in the air. Sincere called his man Smoke over to his black Lexus. Smoke was another member of Big Ray's violent crew. He was tall, probably about 6'4", light-skinned with light brown hair with hazel eyes. He was the pretty-boy type, about twenty-five with a slew of baby mamas. As the two of them sat down in Sincere's car, Sincere told him what was going down. "Yo Smoke. Did you hear what he said?" Smoke lit himself a cigarette, "Hell yeah, I heard what the fuck he said. He said five thousand dollars for killing two crackhead motherfuckers." Sincere shook his head from side to side, "Nah, man." Sincere replied. "He said kill everybody there. You know they have that little girl, man. I ain't killing no little kid, man, especially no little innocent girl." Smoke laughed like he heard a joke. Sincere looked at him and said, "What the fuck you laughing at nigga?" Smoke turned to Sincere and said, "Look, my man, we don't get paid enough anyway to push Big Ray's drugs all day. You do what you want. But I'm beyond mere *carnality*. If I find them, I'm killing everything that moves for five thousand dollars. I'm not leaving nothing there but bittersweet memories," Smoke laughed out loud. Sincere turned and looked at Smoke, "Nigga, what the fuck you said…*carnality*?" Smoke spoke nonchalantly and said, "My man, I ain't no dumb nigga. I'm intelligent. I should've been a lawyer or something like that." They both broke out in laughter as Sincere pulled off into traffic, while he lit up a blunt pondering over the situation in his head.

***

With everything that had happened in my life, it was no wonder why I had changed. I barely went to school. Mom didn't notice. Michele had hit rock bottom. Mom and Steve was a pitiful pair. As I dressed for school, I looked around at my disheveled room for some clean socks. All the clothes on the floor were dirty. At twelve years old, I was pretty much an independent girl. I searched through the pile of dirty clothes to finally find a pair of panties, bra and socks to put on. I could not believe that I was wearing dirty underwear but I was. Hell, I felt dirty so it seemed like a match. As I finished getting dressed in dirty clothes, I reached over on my disheveled dresser for my book bag as a mouse ran right across my feet. I flinched, and then scream at the top of my lungs. I was petrified of mice. I hated them along with bugs. Yeah, I used to be a girly-girl. After I calmed down, I exited out of my dirt hole to the first floor, pass the refrigerator because I knew it was empty. I can't remember the last time Michele went food shopping or cooked, for that matter. I headed toward the front door when I cut my eyes to the side to see Michele sitting in a disarray living room. She looked a hot, hot mess. She was nearly skin-'n-bone. Her long hair was matted and nappy. I don't know when she had gotten a perm last. She looked like she hadn't washed her ass in days. And that wasn't far from the truth because the room smelled like a rat had died in it. The whole house was in shambles.

Michele sat looking hopeless on the couch smoking a Newport 100. Steve was laying on the loveseat with his long legs dangling over the chair. He looked like walking death. Three days earlier he had come home beat up. Word on the streets was that some young dealers had kicked his worthless ass. He had knots on his forehead. Two blackened eyes, busted lip. They broke his nose, ribs, and knocked out his two-front teeth for not paying them for some crack cocaine. Before I left out of the house, I heard Michele yell, "Did you hear me, girl. Make sure you pick me up some cigarettes before you come home." I grimaced, and then slammed the door.

I headed next door to my girl Egypt's house to see if she was going to school. We normally walked to school together, when I did go. Egypt was cool, smart, and down-to-earth. She was about two inches taller than me, brown-skinned, skinny as a rail, with long legs and big feet. She was cute in the face and she had big titties to be so skinny. We had a lot in common especially since both of our mothers were crackheads.

I rang Egypt's doorbell. Within three seconds she appeared at the door dressed in a pair of black spandex leggings and an oversized multi-colored sweater that looked like it came from one of those thrift stores. Her hair was pushed back in a ponytail. And she had on her wired-framed glasses that made her look studious.

"What's up, Egypt?"

"What's up with you, girl?" Egypt asked in her Minnie-Mouse voice.

"Girl, the same ole shit." I said, shaking my head like I was fed up. And I was. I was totally fed up with the way my life had become. I felt I deserved better.

Egypt and I talked, laughed, and giggled on our way to school. I told her about how Steve had gotten his ass kicked by some young dealers. Egypt hated Steve just like she hated her own stepfather Hank. Hank was mean and nasty with his mouth. Hank loved himself some pussy, though. It didn't matter if it was young or old pussy. Pussy was pussy to him. Egypt hated how Steve abused me. I had to tell someone my problems and the only person I had at the time, was her. But I never confided in her about the sexual abuse. About how Steve would come into my bedroom and rape me two to three times a week. I was too ashamed to confide in her about that. It was too painful to admit to her or myself. I guess I felt like she would judge me or look at me differently. I didn't need to be ostracized by her. I needed her to be my friend. I needed someone, anyone other than Michele and Steve. I longed for Angelita to get in touch with me. Write me a letter or send me a postcard. But she never did.

Egypt would always share stories about her family. "Alice, even though I know my mother is a drug addict, thank god, for my grandma. My grandmother helps to take care of me." I listened and cracked a fake smile. I was happy for her, don't get me wrong, but deep down I felt this hollowness opening up inside of me. I had no one. No one I could call up and say, HELP, to. I hadn't seen Randy in years. My grandparents were both deceased. Egypt would often invite me over to her house for dinner. Whenever they had a cookout her grandmother would invite me over to enjoy her hamburgers and hotdogs. If they went to McDonald's or Burger King, they'd invite me too. Sometimes they would pick me up something and save it for me for when I came over to visit. I didn't care if the food was cold, I'd eat it to show my appreciation for thinking of me.

"Girl," I said, "I was hoping you were coming out with something to eat in your hands. We ain't got no food in the house. When is your grandmother coming over?"

"This weekend," Egypt replied.

"Well, I'm hungry so you know where I'm going." I said.

Egypt just looked at me. "Not me. You can go alone, girl. That guy scares me. He always stares at us."

"Well, you can wait outside. I'll go in." I said to her.

Egypt and I walked until we were across the street from the DP gas station on Market Street. "Let's go." Egypt said with this nervous look on her face. Egypt was about to step off she was so scared. "Wait. Wait." I said, "I have to wait for the other guy to come out and pump the gas. Just be cool and wait with me, okay." Egypt nodded her head up and down. All of a sudden three cars pulled up. When the young boy ran out to pump the gas, I ran in the market. This old hairy man with a cane was sitting on a stool. He stared me down and then said, "What you need pretty?" I must admit I was a little startled by him. "Ah, two butter rolls, two Slim Jim's, and two twenty-five cent juices. Oh yeah, and two packs of gum...*Doublemint*."

As the old yellow-skinned man with bushy silver beard was bagging my stuff I asked him if he had a bathroom. "Sure," he replied, "Go straight and make a left, you'll see the door." The more I stared at him the more he kinda looked like that guy Grady on *Sanford and Son*. I stood there with this sulk upon my face. "Is there something wrong," he asked with a face of concern like a sweet daddy would. I batted my eyelashes. "I-I-I was wondering if you could show me." I said in a soft and sensual baby voice. The old man looked me up and down from my feet to my face, slowly, stopped bagging, stood to his feet with his cane, and escorted me to the bathroom; we both walked in and locked the door behind us.

At that moment of us being face-to-face, him standing way above me, he asked, "Can I touch it?" I nodded yes. His wrinkled hand reached for my right nipple and he squeezed it gently. The old man started rubbing harder on my little tits, as he fondled me simultaneously. I added in a moan, here and there to boost his ego. I pulled up my shirt and let him rub my breasts with his hot hands. As he fondled me I remembered the first time I had come to the store. I didn't have enough money for my items. The old man had patted me on the butt and kissed me on the cheek. Then he gave me the things I needed. Since then whenever I was hungry all I had to do was go there and let him feel and touch me for whatever I wanted and needed. But whenever he started to unzip his zipper I'd run out saying, "I have to get to school now." And I'd run out of the store like a bat out of hell. There were only a few patrons waiting but the young gas boy was on the register taking care of business when I came out. The old man bagged my goods and I was on my way.

When Egypt saw me coming out the door, she smiled, but her smile turned upside down when I spun around and ran back into the store. I needed a pack of Newport 100s. I looked at the old man, the old man looked at the young boy, and the young boy looked at me. I tried to ignore them both. I put on my mad-girl face on and rotated my neck as if I was the baddest chick in Paterson. My hands met my small waist, "I said a pack of Newport 100s, please?" As Fred was handing me the cigarettes his face frowned up, "Tell your mother I want my money this week, too!" The young boy stared at the old man with a look of utter disgust on his face as; I dashed out of the store.

As Egypt and I were walking to school, we talked and ate out butter rolls and Slim Jim's. "'Ey, Alice, what do you do to get this stuff all the time?" Egypt said with a peculiar look upon her face. My mouth touched my butter roll but I didn't take a bite. I sighed. "I can't tell you, right now, but one day I will." Egypt just looked at me, while chewing on her butter roll. "You better hide them cigarettes," she said, as we approached school. So I did.

Kids were everywhere. "Look at them two dirty girls." A couple of boys yelled out. "You dirty," I replied in a nasty tone. "At least my mom ain't no crackhead," one nappy-headed boy said. Then all of a sudden, the boys sung in unison, "Alice mother is a crackhead, crackhead, crackhead…" then they ran pass us as one of the boys' said, "And Egypt smells like piss…" Then they all laughed as they ran into the school. Egypt and I paid them stupid boys no attention. As far as I was concerned they had a lot of growing up to do.

***

Months had gone by. It was now spring. Steve and Michele sat on the floor in a dirty, dingy crackhouse. They were a worthless sight. They had been in the crackhouse for 72 hours, straight. Their money was almost gone. Michele had received her check two months earlier, and all they did was smoke coke the last two months.

"Nigga, you turn me on to this shit," Michele snapped. "You fucked me and my daughter's life up. I wished that I never would've met your worthless ass." Steve stood up and blew the crack smoke out, "I told you to let me flip the money, bitch. I told you I could have doubled it. But no, not you, all you wanted to do, was get high. You dirty black bitch!" Michele laid her bony body back and laughed hard as hell in Steve's face. "Nigga, you think I don't know you owe, huh? Nigga, you owe "Big Rayvon" alllll that money. You think the streets ain't talkin', man. Whenever "Big Rayvon" or his goons see you, you are finished, fucked up, a dead nigga. That's what I know, you no-good-black-motherfucker! And *you* think me and my baby leaving town with you, you done lost your goddamn mind!" At first, Steve seemed speechless. Then he pointed at Michele, "Bitch, first of all, I'm leaving with or without your bony ass. And as far as Alice is concerned, what daughter? You ain't no mother, you'a junkie whore bitch who don't care about nothin', but where her next hit of coke is coming from! Look at you, you use to be fine as wine. You had a car, a good job, and a nanny. Now look at you, you ain't got nothin' but that pipe in your hand. And you too busy sucking dick like it is your last day on this earth. When's the last time you saw your *daughter*? She what, 12 maybe 13, you don't even know. Alice out here running around the streets like a grown ass woman," Steve said. Michele staggered to get on her feet. But once she did, she swung her bony arm in Steve's direction aiming for his sunken face. Steve grabbed her arm and spun her around and chokehold her, then slammed her hard against the molded wall. "Bitch, if you ever touch me I'll kill your junkie ass!" Steve stared at her. His eyes drooped and darkened. He pinned her against the wall to make a statement, once he saw the look of fear on her face, he released her from his grip, and walked away.

As Steve was walking away, Michele started yelling at the top of her lungs, talkin' mad shit. Others in the crackhouse paid them two no mind because they knew that they had issues. "Nigga, you gonna pay, you gonna pay. You raped my daughter and pimped her out! You'a rapist, you'a junkie, you ain't nothin', you ain't nothin'." Michele said, slowly sliding down the moldy wall. She began to weep uncontrollably, as two crackheads from across the room yelled, "Shut the fuckup or get the fuck out, bitch, we trying to get our high on." It took time for Michele to compose herself. She hit the pipe again, and then she thought of an idea to get in contact with "Big Rayvon" and collect that $5000.00 she had heard he was offering for Steve's head.

***

I kept ringing the doorbell but there was no answer at Egypt's front door, so I used the key that she had given me just in case this was one of those emergencies. See, Egypt and I felt like we couldn't trust anyone else with our personal business, even though people knew of our moms being junkies. We knew that we couldn't count on anyone but each other. I can't say that I wasn't a little worried when I put the key in the door, because I was scared shitless. I took a deep breath as I walked inside of the house. It was quiet as a mouse. I whispered her name, "Egypt, Egypt," but she never responded to my call. I tiptoed up the stairs to her bedroom. I knocked on the door, once, twice, three times, still no answer. I turned the knob and slowly opened it as it made a squeaking sound. I cut my eyes from side to side afraid that her mom would come out of hiding but she never did. All I could think was that her mom had done something heinous to her. *God, I hoped that she didn't kill the girl and bury her in the basement or backyard*, I thought to myself. Yeah, I had some crazy thoughts roaming through my head. Finally, the door opened enough to see someone sleeping in Egypt's bed. I tiptoed over to the left side of the bed and called out her name again, "Egypt, Egypt," and again she didn't respond. Once I knew that it was Egypt I shook her. Still, she didn't wakeup. This girl sleep too hard, I said to myself. So I got annoyed and shook her again but even harder. "Egypt, Egypt, you sleep?" Egypt was groggy and talking sleepy talk. "Not now," she replied. "You hungry, girl, because I'm starvin'." I said. "Yeah, I'm hungry," she said never opening her eyes. "My grandma didn't bring anything here yet I know there ain't nothing in the kitchen." "Look, girl, I'm going to the DP," I said, "You don't have to come with me, I'll get enough for the both of us, okay. I hope Fred's working today." Egypt chuckled, "I hope his old nasty ass is working too." It was no longer a deep dark secret; I mean I'd finally exposed my bad girl tactics to Egypt. Egypt was silent, at first. One thing I can say was that she never judged me. She never turned her back on me either. She still remained my girl. "Just be careful, girl." Egypt said, and then rolled over to the right side of her twin-sized bed. I knew that Egypt was deathly afraid of Fred, but she didn't knock me for what I did to eat. Little did Egypt know Fred wasn't the only old man, I knew. I had mad skeletons in my closet. I would always find someone to disappear with.

Take for instance, the gym teacher, Mr. Kolinsky at the elementary school. He's this tall, nerdy looking white dude with thick bifocals. He kinda resembled John Lennon. You know, from the Beatles. I'm sure John Lennon was a bit more intellectual than him, though. Anyway, we did the *nasty* multiple times. But he knew just as me that mums were the word. If he fucked up and squealed that was gonna be his ass. I wasn't stupid, by far, I knew that I had to come off bitchy it was the only way I had these niggas believing that I was crazy. They knew a quiet bitch was someone to *watch*, but a crazy bitch was someone to *fear*. I'd ruin Mr. Kolinsky, if he leaked one word. He knew what was up. I didn't think Mr. Kolinsky would do well in jail.

As I stood in front of DP, thinking about what I was going to get, I waited for the young guy to come out to pump the gas. Two cars pulled up to the gas station, and the young guy came running out, as I ran in. Fred smiled when he saw me walk in. Before the door closed this young guy walked in. Fred and I looked at each other, and then cut our eyes at the guy. He was tall, muscular, with a wide nose and thick lips drenched in butter-cream skin. His hair was cut low to the scalp. He looked to be a little older than me. *I've seen him before in the neighborhood every now and then*, I thought to myself. He hung out on the corner with other guys selling weed. I just stood still and waited for him to buy what he needed. The young guy kept staring at me while grabbing some things and then he headed up to the register. He checked his back pants pocket, cut *his* eyes at me, front pockets, cut *his* eyes at me, inner jacket pockets, cut *his* eyes at me, outer jacket pockets, cut *his* eyes at me. Fred was eyeing me down, as he watched the guy doing the same. Fred immediately got annoyed and jealous at the same time. His forehead crumpled up and he had this mean look in his brown eyes. I guess by the guy being much younger than him got the best of him. Fred couldn't bear and grin it any longer so he snapped at the young guy like he was wasting *his* time. "Hurry up! I don't have all day!" Finally, the young guy found his money in the small pocket of his jeans and handed it to Fred. I started heading toward the back of the store. Right away I think the young guy knew what was going down because it was known that Fred was a pervert. Fred nearly broke his neck following me to the bathroom. The young guy pushed the door open to exit out, as he cut his eyes to the back of the store watching me as I reached for the doorknob to the bathroom. The young guy stepped back inside store and yelled, "Yo, c'mere for a minute, pretty thang. C'mere." He said. I didn't know why but I released my hand from the doorknob and walked passed Fred and toward the young guy.

"What's your name?" he asked in a husky tone.

"Alice."

"Are you hungry, Alice?"

Before I could respond he said, "Let's go get something to eat."

I smiled and walked out of the store. Before he walked out of the store he looked back at Fred and put his middle finger up and whispered with this lips, "Fuck you, you pervert. Have a *nice* day." He exited out of the store with a pumped chest and a cocky look upon his face. That was his way of saying: Nigga I just cock blocked your *old* ass.

We walked up to the corner of Park Ave and the young guy and I jumped in a cab.

"Where're we going?" I asked him.

"You like soul food?" He asked me.

I nodded my head up and down.

"Okay, that's where we're going to eat then. Oh, by the way my name is Fat Boy."

"Fat Boy," I repeated for confirmation.

"Yeah, that's what everybody calls me."

"But you're not… *fat*." I said with this perplexed look on my face.

"I was a fat baby. I was always hungry so my mom started calling me Fat Boy. I guess you can say it stuck." He said.

For some reason I felt comfortable in his presence. I felt like I had known him a long time. And in my mind I knew that he knew what I was about to do with Fred. Fat Boy was cool people. Not once did he throw in my face what he saw at the DP gas station, but one thing he did bring to my attention that nearly made me want to bury my head under a rock was that he knew my *mom*. Not only did he know *her*, he knew that she was a *crackhead*. The way he went about telling me was like caressing a toddler who fell and got a boo-boo on her knee: "Yo, I usually see this lady that you remind me of. I mean you look a lot like her. No disrespect, Alice, but I think she might be your mom. I usually see her with this dude named Steve. Everybody in my crew knows Steve. He's a regular. I be seeing them walking around like zombies." I was speechless. My mouth had to be dangling open. My eyes had to be bulging out of their sockets. My face had to be every bit of plum-colored. It was so embarrassing but I tried to cover my shame by smiling. But deep down I was shuddering like a small wounded child. It was hard, real, real hard. I think Fat Boy saw right through me, though.

"It's aiight, Alice," Fat Boy said with this sort of boyfriend assurance, you know what I mean? I mean, like when two people are soulfully connected they feel each other's pain. Well, that's how he made me feel like he understood. Yeah, he made me feel at ease about the whole fucked up situation. "Look, I still live with my mom and stepfather," he said, "And even though my step-father has a good job and pays all the bills for our household, he still has mad issues. He's a functional alcoholic and as a result of the alcohol it changed him into an abuser. Yeah, he used to beat on my mom like crazy." I grew to hate the man. Fat Boy had this cutting look in his eyes. Then within a few seconds he resumed back, nodding his head up and down while biting on his bottom lip. I remained quiet because I could tell that it was like a flesh wound that hadn't fully healed. "See that's why I do my own thing. Make my own money. I never asked my step-father for a shit." He said in a curt tone. Yeah. It was obvious that he was still teed off about the situation. I didn't blame him nor did I try to make light of it. It was pretty fucked up.

Fat Boy had guts for a fifteen year old. I mean working the corners selling weed was not an easy hustle. There was a lot to lose like freedom for one. But I fully understood where he was coming from. Weed allowed him to take care of himself. And using the assets that God had blessed me with allowed me to do the same. Yeah, we seemed to have more in common than I'd thought. We were young and independent, both trying to fill that empty void.

It was about noon when we stepped foot inside of Eva-Mae's Soul Food Restaurant near the Boys & Girls Club over on 21st Avenue. We helped ourselves to a table. Minutes later this skinny ass waitress with long kinky, sporting a mini-skirt and a tank top with some white and pink K-Swiss sneakers on, came over popping chewing gum, ghetto as hell, and asked us what we wanted to order. Instead of us ordering lunch, we ordered the dinner special.

I took it upon myself to order, first. Huh. When it came to food, *Alice Banks is not shy*, I thought to myself. "Um, I'll have fried chicken with macaroni and cheese and potato salad. "Yeah, and um, I'll have the same with a side of string beans."

"Ya'll, want anything to drink, what about dessert?" She asked, chewing like a cow.

I looked over at Fat Boy. "Get whatever you want, girl."

"Coke. Apple pie, please?"

Fat Boy interjected, "Make that two slices."

After the waitress jotted everything down, she walked away, still popping that damn chewing gum.

I twisted my lips a little reluctant to ask Fat Boy a question. But I found the courage to do it anyway. "Um, can I take some of this food home?" "I thought you were hungry," he asked. "I am. It's not for me; it's for my friend, Egypt. I just wanted to bring her something, if you don't mind."

Fat Boy started laughing.

"Why are you laughing at me?" I asked, somewhat offended.

"Nah. I'm not laughing at you, just… It's cool. I'll order something for you to take home to your friend. I got you. And if you want something else, let me know."

Honestly, I could not believe that this was happening. I mean it had been some time since I had someone who treated me this nice.

We talked and laughed until our food arrived. Finally, our food was served piping hot. I didn't even bother to say grace as I have been taught. I just started digging in. But in the back of my mind, I wondered what Fat Boy would want in place of the free meal.

Before leaving the restaurant, Fat Boy was kind enough to order Egypt the same meal we ate. He left the waitress a small tip, and we headed out. Fat Boy held another cab, and we jumped in. While seating in the backseat I kept wondering when Fat Boy was going to make his move on me. But he never did.

"So, Alice, where are we dropping you off at?" Fat Boy asked.

Is he for real, I thought to myself? *He's really going to take me home?*

"Home."

"And where is that?"

"Over on the east side of town, near 33rd." I said, a little hesitant in letting him know where I lived.

He cut his eyes at me, and sucked his teeth. "Girl, what's the address?"

"Oh, 331."

"You have a cell phone?" he asked me.

"No."

"Yo, taxi man, you have a piece of paper and a pen?" Fat Boy leaned forward and reached for the paper and pen. "I'ma give you my cell phone number, call me anytime you want to. If you can't call, come up on my block, aiight."

"Okay, Fats, I mean, Fat Boy."

The taxi driver pulled up to my yellow house. I thought Fat Boy was going to get out and escort me to my front door, maybe ask to come in for some Alice-dessert, but he didn't. As I was exiting out of the taxi, Fat Boy smacked me on my butt, and then he said with a smirk on his face, "And stay away from the DP station too, aiight."

"Okay." I smiled, and closed the door to the cab.

I headed toward Egypt's house. The smell of food woke Egypt up before I had a chance to. By the time I walked into her bedroom, she was already sitting up. "Girl, that food smells good. Where you get that food from, Alice?" I handed it to her, and told her the whole story from the time I had left her house. Ten minutes into the story, Egypt pursed her lips and yelled, "FAT BOY, FAT BOY from the corner?! Girlllll, don't he mess wit' crazy Nicole?"

"I don't know," I replied, somewhat annoyed by her telling me about this chick.

While Egypt was steady stuffing her face she kept on running off at the mouth. "Yo, Alice that girl stabbed two girls at school and they said it was over Fat Boy."

Did I ask her to give me the 411 on this chick named Nicole; no, she volunteered the information and that really ticked me off! "Well, that's her problem." I said, and continued on with my conversation, without a care in the world. I was talking so fast I never really let Egypt get a word in edgewise. I just kept on rambling about how nice; this new prince charming was to me. If it was puppy love, I didn't know or care. No one had been that nice to me in a long time.

***

Michele sat in the backseat with Smoke. In the front seat sat "Big Rayvon" and Sincere. "You did say that I would get $5000.00, if I show you where Steve's at, right?" Smoke smugly said, "You get the money when you show us where he's at." Then Sincere jumped in and said, "When he get home call this number," he handed it to her, "and say: *he didn't come home yet*. That's all you have to say and then hang up. Make sure you call from a payphone. Now write your address down and give the paper to Smoke. Don't forget to call from a payphone, not a house phone. Leave the doors unlocked and make sure he doesn't leave."

"How am I 'sposed to make sure he doesn't leave if I'm at the payphone, huh?"

There was dead silence.

"When do I get my money, Big Ray?" Michele asked, fidgeting in the bloody-red leather seat.

Big Ray never even blinked or turned his head to respond. He never said one word the whole time she was in the car. Smoke stared at her, "Look, I told you before; as soon as it's done you'll get your money." Big Ray cut his eyes over at Sincere and Sincere cut his eyes back at Smoke. Smoke dug in his pants pocket and handed Michele ten vials of crack cocaine and a twenty-dollar bill. They stopped the car and Michele opened the door and flew out of the car. "Damn, I'm glad that bitch is gone. She smells like dead fish and shit mixed together. Damn! Roll down the window, Big, it stinks back here." Smoke scrunched up his nose. Sincere burst out laughing. "Oh shit! Big, go back around the corner I forgot to tell her to make sure the girl ain't there. Damn!" Smoke popped his forehand and sucked his teeth. Finally, Big Ray spoke in a loud menacing tone, "Like I told you before, if *Jesus* is in that house kill him too. Bitch think she's getting paid, kill her first. That *bitch* smoked up my shit, too!"

***

It had been three weeks since I had went to eat with Fat Boy. I was avoiding him every since I heard about his crazy ass girlfriend Nicole. I had seen him two other times but he didn't see me. He had sent a message with a friend to tell me to call him but I hadn't called. As I was leaving Egypt's house to go home and get a change of clothes I had this sad look on my face. "Girl, why don't you just go ahead and call him because I'm tired of seeing you look like that."

"Shut up, Egypt. I'll be back later." I said, as I was exiting out of her bedroom.

***

Michele was sitting on the couch in the living room drinking a 22.ounce Natural Ice, when she heard knocks at the door. She rose to her feet with the beer still in her hands and whispered with her mouth against the door, "Who is it?" A male voice answered back, "It's me, baby...Steve." Oh, shit! She said to herself. She hadn't seen Steve since the fight at the crackhouse. As she unlocked and opened the door the only thing that crossed her mind was to call Big Ray and his goons.

"Hey Lady, how you been?" Steve said.

Michele took one good, hard look at him and scrunched up her nose. He looked like shit. "I'm alright, Steve, how you been?" Steve stepped inside smelling like piss and shit mixed together. "Listen Michele, I'm sorry about the things I said to you. And I'm sorry for putting my hand on you, too. I was wrong and I'm man enough to admit it." Steve entered the living room and sat down on the couch. He dumped about five crack vials on the coffee table. They talked and smoke; all the while Michele was trying to figure out a way to get to the payphone. She no longer gave a fuck about Steve; he messed up big time as far as she was concerned.

"Damn, I need another beer. You want one?" She asked Steve.

"Hell yeah, I got some change." Steve said, as he reached in his dingy pants pocket and pulled out all these coins: quarters, nickels, pennies and dimes as they spread out all over the coffee table. "You want me to run to the corner store?" he asked.

"What…just don't smoke everything up from me, nigga. No, I'll go." Michele and Steve both started laughing, and then she fled out of the door.

***

I walked into the house only to find *Steve* sitting in our living room. Instantly, a grimace appeared on my face. I hadn't seen him in three weeks and that was fine with me. I rolled my eyes at him and started to head upstairs to my bedroom. "Well, hello, to you too miss thang," I heard Steve say as I was climbing the stairs. I completely ignored him. I turned the knob to my bedroom; stepped inside, and quickly slammed the door behind me, shivering like crazy. I sat on my bed, feeling my eyes tearing up. Just seeing Steve brought back painful memories. I lay across my bed, grabbed my pillow, wrapped my arms around it, and cried.

***

Michele hands were shaking as she pressed each number on the payphone. "Hello? Hello?" "Yeah, who is this?" Sincere asked. Michele was nervous as hell. "He didn't come home." She said, and then hung up the phone and headed toward the liquor store. Sincere and Smoke, were together when he received the tip. "That's the call, you ready?" Smoke didn't hesitate to respond, "Hell yeah, let's go before he leaves." They jumped in Sincere's car and sped off. Michele entered the house with a brown paper bag in her hands. Steve was still chillin' in the living room, with his stinky feet propped up on the coffee table. Michele joined him in the living room. Steve never told Michele that Alice had come home. Michele handed Steve a 22.ounce Budweiser and then she picked up the pipe that Steve had ready. She was jittery as she kept eyeing the door. Every sound she heard made her nearly jump out of her skin. Steve popped opened his beer and leaned back and watched Michele try to hold the fire to the stem. Sweat was profusely trickling down her face like a sick dope fiend.

"You all right," Steve asked her.

"Yeah, I'm okay. Just a little under the weather. I think I'm coming down with something."

"Well, take a blast of that pipe it'll make you feel better." Steve told her. Then Steve had a thought and shared it with Michele. "Um, baby, why we don't go to a rehab and get clean. We can get our lives back on track and move out of this fucking city. I'm serious. Let's get clean together. My mom called a couple of centers to check the availability for me, yesterday. What you think about it, baby?" Steve looked over at Michele and then took a long swig of beer waiting for her to respond. Michele disregarded his question. She was too busy waiting for everything to go down.

There was silence between Michele and Steve for what seemed like four minutes. The sound of the wall clock ticking was the only noise heard. Then suddenly the front door swung open and Smoke and Sincere stormed in with pistols in their hands. Michele jumped up and pointed her index finger toward Steve. Her voice was crackling as she spoke, "Th-e-r-e he-he…" POW! POW! Two bullets hit her in the face. Blood splattered all over the walls, couch, coffee table, ceiling, and floor. Sincere's hand was steady as he pointed the pistol at her as she fell backwards and hit the floor with loud thump. Steve stood shaking nearly shitting in his pants. Smoke grabbed Steve. Steve screamed like a little bitch, "Please…don't kill me! Please…don't kill me, man, please!" Smoke pistol-whipped Steve. Then he beat Steve over the head, WHACK, WHACK, WHACK, with his gun trying to knock him into oblivion. Smoke yelled to Sincere, "Yo, man, go check the rest of the house." Smoke continued to beat Steve senselessly, "You think you can steal from Big Ray, nigga!" Steve's body was limp and wobbling like a wino. "Please don't kill me!" WHACK, WHACK, WHACK! Steve's eyes were so swollen he could barely open them. His nose was broken and bloodied. His jaw was broken, lip busted with ripe blood oozing out of it. His head was the size of a basketball and blood was dribbling down his face onto the dingy white shirt he had on. He was also slightly incoherent. Steve's words slurred as his dark black lips trembled, "P-p-p-p-l-l-eeaase!!!"

***

I heard this popping sound. I swore it sounded like firecrackers or maybe gunshots but I wasn't sure. I rose from my bed and hid in the closet because suddenly I grew afraid. I kneeled down with my back against the wall, whimpering. I was so scared I nearly pissed in my pants. I heard what sounded like footsteps heading upstairs and then someone opened the door to my bedroom. Someone walked into my room. I was heaving, trying to bury my head between my legs. Someone walked toward the walk-in closet and swung open the doors and found me cowering in the corner. I was shaking, so afraid. This young man locked eyes with me, while I continued to cry with snot running down my nose. I knew that something bad was going on downstairs. This man put one of his fingers up to his lips advising me to be quiet, as he stood there with his right arm extending out with his gun pointed right at my head. I was still as the air. Then I heard another man break the silence by yelling out, "Yo, Sincere, anybody up there?" The man paused and then responded with his eyes piercing mine. "Nah. Nobody else here." He yelled out and closed the closet doors, and then walked out of the bedroom and headed back downstairs. I took a deep, deep breath and balled my quivering body, tightly along the shaggy hunter-green rug; tears flooded my eyes and streamed down the side of my face, as I wondered if my mom was dead or alive.

Smoke stood over Steve's broken, beaten, and bloodied body. "Have a safe trip," he said, while plugging three bullets in his head. Then they both jetted out of the door and into Sincere's getaway car and sped off.

**

I sat on the floor with my legs bent and my face wedged in-between my knees, for what seemed like ten minutes. My hands were balled up into fists, squeezing the sides of my face together. My body was shaking and I was crying uncontrollably. Finally, I got up on my knees and peeped out the closet door. I didn't see or hear anything, so I eased out of the closet and grabbed my satchel that my mom had brought me one Christmas. I started grabbing clothes and what little I had to stuff into the bag. I paused, as I was shoving the clothes in the bag because I thought I had heard sirens, but I wasn't sure. My hands were quivering so badly. God, I was so scared. I slowly tiptoed from the dresser to the door, opened it slowly and peeped out. There was no one there, so I took one step out of the door, and then another. But suddenly I realized I had forgotten something so I ran back inside my bedroom, slightly lifted my mattress and grabbed a picture and a piece of paper. I kept cutting my eyes from side to side; my body was shivering so badly. I took a deep breath to try to calm myself down, and then I eased back out of my bedroom, and headed downstairs.

When I got down to the kitchen, the first thing I saw was Steve. Immediately, I started shaking. With nervousness running through my body, I cut my eyes to the right of the room, then the left of the room, and I saw my mom laying on her back with half of her face blown off. My eyes grew wide as I dropped my bag and grabbed my stomach as I vomited all over the floor. The sound of the sirens were getting closer and closer, louder and louder. I bent down feeling the sickest I'd ever felt and grabbed my bag as I noticed the floor was covered with blood. As I was running toward the door, my sneakers made a smacking sound like I was running through shallow waters. Just the sound of the blood against the soles of my sneakers made me vomit again once I got outside. It was the worst sound in the world, and the reality of me stepping through my mom's blood was a memory I'd never forget.

I passed Egypt's house and ran down the street to the payphone. Once I got to the payphone I pulled from my bag the piece of paper. I used one of my forefingers to press the ten-digits, as I looked down at my bag, then my shirt, pants, and sneakers, I noticed I had blood on me. I can't tell you how that made me feel, to have my mother's blood on me. I wanted to just die right there in that payphone booth. Just die, right then and there.

The phone rang, and as it rang I wept, louder and louder, still shaking like a leaf. Ring, ring, ring… as I was about to hang-up, someone picked up.

"Hello? Hello?"

"Fat Boy, Fat Boy, its Alice. I need to see you, please…it's an emergency," my voice was crackling with each and every word I spoke. "What's wrong, are you okay, you sound frazzled. I'm home can you come here?" he asked. "Yeah, yeah, that's cool. What's your address?" Fat Boy told me his address, but he told me to meet him in a discreet location that we were both familiar with, which was near this barbershop over on Beech Street. I held the first taxi I saw, jumped in. The taxi driver noticed how shaken up I was. He also noticed the blood on my shirt. "Mami, you all right?" he asked in a Hispanic accent. "Yeah, yeah," I said, looking down at my sneakers. The driver left me alone. I arrived at the discreet location within fifteen minutes. I was so scared to even get out of the car.

As I was getting out of the taxi, I noticed Fat Boy standing across the street with a navy-blue hoodie on. One of his hands was buried in his pocket and the other hand was holding a lit blunt. When Fat Boy laid eyes on me, he could tell that something bad had happened. Of course the *blood* was a dead giveaway. I nearly collapsed in his arms. Fat Boy caught me, wrapped his arm around my waist and cautiously we walked to his house.

Fat Boy lived in a row-house complex. He opened the door and carefully guided me in the spacious living room and helped me sit down on the leather maroon couch. "Don't worry, Alice, nobodies here but my little sister. Both of my parents are working second shift." I was a bucket of water; I couldn't stop crying to save my life. "Listen, maybe you'll feel better if you clean yourself up." he said, as he walked toward a closet door, then walked back over to me and handed me a washcloth and towel and a fresh bar of his mother's Dove soap. He then guided me to the upstairs bathroom to take a hot shower. "There's some lotion on the top shelf, Alice," he said, as he was shutting the door behind him.

As the door closed, I stood there staring at my reflection. The blood on my shirt made me lean over and throw up in the toilet. I felt so sick, so sad, and so angry. God. I had so many different emotions running through me. Tears flowed down my face as I peeled off my soiled clothing, untied my shoelaces, and stepped out of my bloody sneakers. I tossed everything in the small trashcan. I turned the nozzle to the shower on, listened to the water sprout out of the showerhead. It sounded like rain to my ears. I stepped in the shower and let the hot water drench me from my head down to my toes. I wanted the water to take me away, make me disremember what was happening to me. In the split second, I wished my life were how it used to be with Michele and me. Why? Why? Why? God. I needed to know why this happened to us, to me, and how was I ever going to recover…how?

My train of thought was distracted as I heard Fat Boy asking me through the door what I wanted to drink. I couldn't think straight, so I didn't respond. My mind was all mangled with frustration, anger, sorrow, and emptiness. My mother was dead. Dead! She was all I had in this world, and she was dead.

After I finished taking my shower, I stepped out of the bathroom in a sky-blue long T-shirt that read: Pretty Thang in dark blue letters, still shaken up. I inhaled the scent of weed lingering from a bedroom off to the far right. Fat Boy stepped out as he heard me shut the bathroom door. "Oh, you could've left it open. C'mere." I walked toward Fat Boy and entered his cozy bedroom with posters of Tupac, Biggy, Jay-Z, and Lil' Kim plastered on his white walls. "Have a seat," he said, inviting me to have a seat on his bed. I sat on the edge, still shaking in my skin. "I'll be right back. Let me go check on, Jada." "How old is your sister," I asked as he was heading out the bedroom door. "Five. Her babysitter Donna didn't show up so I had to watch her tonight." Then he disappeared from my sight.

***

"Hey, Ja," Fat Boy said in a soft tone. Jada smiled, as he covered her little feet with her Dora blanket and changed the channel on the TV to Nickelodeon so that she could watch her favorite cartoons. He exited out of the room. He then, walked downstairs to the kitchen and grabbed two cookies out of the canister and poured a small glass of milk, then headed back upstairs to Jada's room. "Here you go, little one. Here's a little snack before bed." "Thank you, brother." She said in her small baby voice. Fat Boy placed the milk on her princess nightstand and handed her the two cookies in her little chocolate hands. "I'll be in my room if you need me, okay." Jada nodded her head up and down. He kissed her on the forehead and stood to head to the door. "Marlon," Jada said. "What Jada?" "Who that in your room?" she asked. "Eat your cookies and watch TV, don't worry about that, okay, big head, and don't say nothing to mommy either. I'll buy you some candy tomorrow, aiight." Jada looked at him with her big brown doe-eyes, and smiled. "Okay, and you got a big head." She said, followed by an adorable laugh. Fat Boy exited out of her bedroom and returned back to his, only to find Alice stretched out on his bed.

***

I was still wide-awake. I couldn't sleep, even if I tried to. The grisly scene was stuck in my head. I couldn't seem to block it out. I wiped the tears from my eyes with my left backhand, as Fat Boy stood in silence. He kept staring at me. It made me feel so uncomfortable. I knew what he wanted to know, but probably didn't know how to come out and ask, especially with me in my fragile condition. So I volunteered the information, just to keep him at ease and me in good hands until I figured out what to do next. I needed Fat Boy in the worst way, and I think deep down he knew it too. Here I was twelve going on thirteen. He was fifteen acting like he was twenty-five coming to my rescue.

"C'mere." I said, asking him to have a seat.

I sat up, sighed, maybe three times before telling him what I had witnessed—Michele and Steve lying in a pool of their own blood, shot dead. I broke down every time I mentioned their names. Every thought of them, the house, the guy who found me in the closet, the gun, the blood, seeing half of my mom's face blown away. It gave me the creeps. Fat Boy remained quiet the whole time I told him the story. He just shook his head at certain parts, but when I told him about my mom, his eyes froze and this mean look appeared in his eyes. At that point, I knew that he really cared about my wellbeing and me. I can't tell you how safe and secure he made me feel.

Fat Boy was turning sixteen in a couple of days. For it to be mid-July, the weather was mild, on occasions, not scalding hot where you were unable to stand it. Fat Boy was very street savvy for his age, unlike myself. It didn't take a rocket scientist to figure out that the cops would be looking for me. And once they did find me, and found out that I was at the scene of the crime and had left, they'd probably consider me a suspect. I had so many thoughts rushing through my head. I knew that they would most definitely want to talk to me. But, my biggest worry was Fat Boy. I didn't want to get him caught up in the mix. I didn't want them to think that he was a part of this madness either. I wanted to keep him safe as well as myself.

"Alice, try and relax. Girl, you are a bundle of nerves. Take a nap. Shut your eyes and go to sleep. Don't worry; I'll take care of you. Everything is going to be okay." He pulled the covers over my quivering body, and as he did, he had a distant look in his eyes like he was remembering something. "When I was little my grandmother taught me that when I was afraid of the bogeyman or whenever something bad had happened to say this prayer…" he closed his eyes and began to recite the Lord's Prayer:

"Our Father, who art in heaven,
hallowed be thy name.
Thy Kingdom come,
thy will be done,
on earth as it is in heaven
Give us this day our daily bread.
And forgive us our trespasses,
as we forgive those who trespass against us.
And lead us not into temptation,
but deliver us from evil.
For thine is the kingdom,
the power and the glory,

for ever and ever.
Amen."

As I was drifting to sleep, I wondered why Fat Boy had prayed for me. *Why would a drug dealer be praying?* I thought to myself. It seemed weird. I mean, I thought drug dealers were fearless people. I thought that they were like atheist, that they had no faith or belief in a Higher power. That's what I thought up until that day. The thought of asking Fat Boy to teach me that prayer was on the tip of my tongue, but I couldn't find the words to ask. Nope. For some reason the words "teach me" seemed cemented to my tongue.

***

The Banks residence was swamped with blue uniforms surrounding the premises. The street was blocked off with bright yellow barricades. The house was taped off with thick yellow "caution" ribbon. People were standing across the street, peeping out their windows, or standing on their front porches, wondering what had happened. Sirens were bellowing, crimson lights were swirling, walkie-talkies and police radios were like music in the neighborhood. Egypt was standing on her front porch biting her nails with tears streaming down her face. She just had a gut feeling that something terrible had happened to Alice. A few minutes later, her mom, Virginia came out on the porch in her dingy pajamas.

"Listen, this is Detective Simon Springs, send Homicide and Forensics to 331 East 33rd Street, we have a double-homicide here." He stood in his 6'4" medium-built frame and pulled off his cap, rubbed his bald head, and placed his cap back on, and then turned to his partner of five years John Benny and said, "This looks like a hit was put on these two." "Definitely drug-related. I mean they left the evidence on the kitchen table." Detective Benny said as he pierced the scene with his bright blue eyes and lifted off his cap to scratch the right side of his blonde hair. Detective Springs nodded his head and massaged his dark-skinned face. "I want every inch of this house dusted for prints. You find anything let me know right away." He told Detective Benny. "Will do." Detective Benny replied, and then walked his 6'2" muscular frame over to inform the other officers, while he took a look around for himself. "'Ey Springs," Detective Benny called out. "Yeah." Detective Springs responded as he was looking at the front door. "You may want to take a look at these prints here in the kitchen." Detective Benny said. Detective Springs ambled into the kitchen to find footprints in the blood. "Looks like someone left in a hurry, huh?" Detective Springs said. "Get forensics on it ASAP. I'll be outside asking the neighbors some questions."

Detective Springs walked out of the premises, looked to his left and then to his right when he noticed Egypt and this thin woman standing on the front porch. He had a hunch that maybe Egypt knew something by the way she was crying and he also noticed the woman standing beside her *wasn't* trying to console her. "Excuse me, ma'am, I don't mean to interrupt you but did you happen to know the Banks?" He asked, while discreetly observing Egypt's body language. He noticed how nervous she was. How she couldn't stop biting her nails. How she didn't make eye contact with him. Tears just poured from Egypt's eyes. He cuts his eyes over to the woman who stood about 5'9" and listened to her *try* to explain the relationship between Egypt and the *girl*. "My daugr was the bes of friends wit' Alist." She said as she twisted her discolored lips. Virginia was incoherent. That was the first thing Detective Springs noticed about her. The second thing was how she looked. She looked like she had just gotten out of bed. The third thing he observed was her hair. Her long, blond weave was disheveled and matted. He noticed that she had crust in the inner corners of her brown eyes. He noticed how her coffee complexion was ashy like it hadn't been washed in days. And how she was still in her pajamas that barely fit her bony frame. Detective Springs had a flustered look upon his thirty-year-old face. "Excuse… ah, you mentioned, *Alice*," he said. Virginia nodded her head as she repeated herself again. "Alist and my daugr were bes friends. Alist lived-ed there wit' her mom, Chell, I mean Mechel and her mom's nigga Steve." Detective Springs observed Egypt's mom especially how her words slurred, her eyes drooped, and how fidgety she was as he jotted the names: Alice, Michele, and Steve down in his pocket notepad. "Can you describe Alice to me? Or…" He looked at Egypt as she looked at him with sadness in her eyes. "Or maybe you might have a picture of her." Egypt nodded her head up and down, still crying her heart out and headed back inside to find a picture. A male voice came over his radio, "Detective Springs, please?" "Excuse me, ma'am. Yeah, this is Springs…" Egypt returned back downstairs with a picture in her quivering hands. She extended her long arm out and Detective Springs reached in for the photo. He noticed that Egypt was trying to say something, while he was on the radio, so he cut the conversation short. Egypt opened her mouth, then took a deep breath, "Sir, I know who was in the house after they were shot. It was Alice." She lowered her head barely able to compose herself. Tears continued to pour from her weary eyes onto her yellow T-shirt. Detective Springs kneeled down and looked Egypt in her young eyes and said, "How do you know for sure that it was Alice?" Egypt sniffled a couple of times, "Because she was here with me, then she went home to get a change of clothes, but she never came back. She-she-she never came back!" Egypt lost control as she witnessed two black body bags being hauled out of the home. She ran back into the house in hysterics. Detective Springs noticed how Egypt's mom didn't try to excuse herself to console her distraught daughter. She stood on the porch seemingly in a world of her own. "Miste, can you tels me wha happened. Who got hurt?" she asked. Detective Springs sighed, "Ma'am, I'm not at liberty to say." His eyes lowered to the picture of Alice as he felt this soft spot in his heart to find this missing little girl. "If you or your daughter happen to remember anything, please…Ah, do you mind, if I ask for your work number," he said. She shifted her body and stood on her right leg barely able to stand straight. "I'm not workin'. I'm on welfare," she replied. "Well, here is my card. Call if you remember anything, okay. Thanks for your time." He watched her body language, as she was still fidgety and then stepped off the porch and headed back to the crime scene.

***

On the other side of town, Sincere and Smoke sat before Big Ray. "It's a done deal," Smoke said, "They won't be stealing from nobody else, that's fo' sure. We blasted both of 'em fools. Three to the head and now they're dead." He laughed. Big Ray just sat back marinating Smoke's words, while sipping on his tall glass of orange juice with an expressionless look upon his chubby face. "We still get that money, right, Big Ray?" Sincere asked. Big Ray cut his right eye over at his bodyguard; this tall deep-dark-skinned man dressed in all black standing behind him and nodded his head. The bodyguard walked over to the safe that was behind a picture on the wall and within a minute's time he cracked it open. He pulled out a gun and a stack of money. He tossed the money on the marble table. "Keep your mouths shut 'bout this, stay low for a minute too. Go to Atlantic City or somewhere. And don't be telling no fucking body 'bout what went down here. If you do your mama is going to be looking for a black dress." Big Ray said with a stern look on his face. Sincere leaned forward ad picked up the cash and him and Smoke walked out. As they shut the door behind them, the muscular bodyguard turned to Big Ray and said; "I hope you're not making a mistake by letting them live." Big Ray stood to his feet and as he was walking his stout body toward the big window, he said, "Nah. It's cool. They make too much money for me. But if you hear anything, let me know because I can't afford to have any loose ends. If the cops start sniffin' they gonna know I'm behind this. Those two little niggas loyal, why take a chance. There aren't any witnesses anyway. Smoke said it was only those two junkies there." Big Ray gazed out of the window admiring the City in which he corrupted with a smug look upon his face.

***

Fat Boy towel dried his chiseled young body. He dabbed a little body oil on his chest area and down by his navel. He put on a wife beater T and a pair of plaid boxers and a pair fresh white sweat socks. Slipped his sized eleven's in his slippers and exited out of the steamy bathroom. He walked into his bedroom to find me snuggled underneath the white comforter balled in a fetal position. He slipped into bed with me, feeling the heat from my hot nude body through the thin fabric of his shirt. I think, then, was when he realized I could be no more than thirteen or fourteen years old. He gaped at me while I attempted to go to sleep, admiring me up close and personal as he whispered in my ear. "You are so damn beautiful, girl." I didn't feel beautiful. I felt ugly and emotionless. Deep within I felt like a motherless child desperately yearning to be held and loved.

Fat Boy got closer to me, able to smell the oil sheen in my hair, and sniffed the smell of Dove off of my supple skin. He pecked his soft lips on my neck, then my earlobe teasing my ear with his teeth, biting me softly until I finally raised my head and turned to face him. We gazed into each other's eyes and I felt this sparkle in my heart. He moved in closer and kissed me so gently that I felt butterflies swarming around in my tummy. I had never given myself to anyone, willingly. Steve had *raped* me numerous times. I used to just lie there, numb with tears purging from my eyes. The thought of him selling me to the Dempsey left a nasty taste in my mouth. Steve pimped me out to drug dealers, junkies, anyone who was willing to satisfy his needs. Deep down I knew nothing about love and softness. I knew nothing about passion, compassion, and love or like. Everything that came to me was forced and manhandled, manipulative, and dismantled me to their liken, not mine. I had no say. No voice. No choices. I was just their puppet dangling from a long frayed string waiting to fall to my demise. I was used up and spat out and tossed to the side like road kill.

I felt myself breathing erratically. Feeling Fat Boy's body so close to mine was a feeling I had never experienced before. I felt this desire, this impulse, this unfamiliar feeling racing through my veins. God, I wanted him and I wanted him to want me too. I wanted what we wanted to be gentle and endearing and memorable. For the first time, I wanted to be touched, loved, and retouched for as long as he wanted to feel my pain and suffering.

When our lips met, I felt a deep chemistry between us. The feel of his moist lips against mine, his tongue tasting like mint toothpaste swirled around in my mouth. I wanted to tie our tongues together like a shoelace. I didn't want to part away from him. I gazed at his muscular body, scrolling him from his socks to his face. His right hand reached in for my face and pulled me closer to him. I licked his earlobe, pecked his cheek, above his eye, and forehead. His left hand massaged my left nipple until hit hardened. His moved himself slowly down to my left breast and licked it in a circular motion. The feel of his warm saliva against my skin sent chills up and down my body. I felt myself get moist. My clit was throbbing, hungry. I wanted him but I didn't want to move too fast. I wanted him to be in control. Slowly my legs parted as he eased down in-between my legs. He raised his arms and pulled off his wife beater T. Then he eased out of his boxers and flung them on the chair next to the door. He leaned over where I could see how broad his shoulders were. He was beautiful all coated in his flawless butter-cream skin. Simply fuckin' beautiful to marvel at. Gently he eased down and with both thumbs as he parted my moist lips. My clit was fully exposed as he licked it so meticulously. My back arched, lifting from the bed, my mouth opened and sound came out like moans and ah's and ooh's. His tongue made beautiful love to my pussy. The heels of my feet raised and rested on his smooth back as he licked me deeper and harder, deeper and harder. My hands gripped the pillow, tongue swept across my enamel, then my lips to make them gloss of saliva. "You taste sweet like strawberries," he said, while moving up to my navel, then my breasts as he licked and pulled on them with his teeth. He raised his body slightly, face-to-face, mouth-to-mouth, eyes to eyes, and then he placed his hand on his manhood and gently inserted it in my sodden hole. The feel of his hard penis sent electric shock waves throughout my body. His motions were like waves, a rhythm of slow pumps deep inside of me. My eyes were rolling back in my head. My fingers gripped the pillow and sheets as he slowly pumped me. His warm hands lifted my ass up to get a better feel as he pumped me a little faster, in-between he whispered, "Am I hurting you?" I swayed my head against the pillow, and managed to ease out, "No. You make me feel beautiful. I never felt like this before..." His rhythm was steady and precise and so satisfying. "Turn over." I said in a soft-spoken tone. As we switched positions, I was slithering down to his dick and before I could put the bulging *head* in my mouth, Fat

Boy stopped me. "No." he said softly, " You don't have to do that to me. I'm not *them*. Don't do *me* like them. Baby, you're not a slut, whore, bitch, or skank, you hear me. Don't let those niggas taint you. Make *love* to *me*, Alice. Let me *feel* your soul. Let me *taste* your spirit. I tasted yours and it tasted soooo good." Then he closed his eyes and licked his lips. *Dammmmnnnnn*, that shit he said sounded so fly and sexy to my ears. That was some R. Kelly shit he was saying to me. And I felt it. I felt it deep —deeper than deep. Fat Boy had me open--wide fuckin' open.

It took everything in me to give him what he had asked for…everything. Every bad thought I had, I had to block out of my head. Every bad experience, I blocked it out. Every bad taste in my mouth, I pretended it tasted sweet like raw sugar. And then I closed my eyes and pictured myself as this other girl—this sweet innocent girl—this girl who hadn't lost her virginity. This girl who was experiencing love, not fucking, for the very first time. I kept picturing her until I felt like her. I climbed on top of him and ogled at his handsome face. I raised my ass and slowly lowered myself onto his penis hearing wetness slip and slide up and down his long hard dick. God, he felt like six inches or more inside of me. He felt delicious to my flesh. My body was overcome with elation for him. I widened my legs and it felt soooo good! His hands gripped the headboard and I rode him deeper and deeper inside of me. We were both pumping in a rapid cadence. All of a sudden I felt something I'd never felt before. A sudden surge of ecstasy, an extra good feeling explored throughout my body. Fat Boy gripped my ass motioning me to pump harder and harder. The feeling was soooo intense. I squeezed my pelvis, moaned so full of delight, as we shook and I let out a long sensual scream as his body shuddered and a raise of his right hand met my mouth and muffled the sound of me reaching my peak of orgasm. It was the first time I'd ever come without feeling dirty after. Fat Boy was the first to have made love to me. And for that I was indebted to him on many levels.

As morning broke, I heard footsteps heading upstairs. I nudged Fat Boy with my pointy elbow, as his sleepy eyes struggled to open. I said, "I think your *parents* are home." His eyes widened as he leaped out of bed and so did I. I hid in his closet as he wrapped himself in his white bathrobe and exited out of his bedroom door. I sat on the closet floor until he returned back. When he opened the closet door, I was cowered in the corner of his closet juddering so full of grief. Tears were streaming down my face like a downpour of hard rain. I had relived the scene all over again. Fat Boy picked me up off the floor and carried me back to his bed, where he held me so tenderly until my eyes slowly shut as my mind drifted back to us making love snuggled in his dreamy arms.

***

For the next six months, I never left Fat Boys side, unless he was going to work the corners with his crew. Most of the time I'd hang low, especially when his parents were home. We had a signal for the coast was clear. Two rings: meant chill a little longer. Three rings: meant meet me at our discreet location, which was at the library's basement in the children's room. Nobody would suspect to find us there. Eventually Fat Boy knew that he would have to figure another solution out, especially when the weather and fall and winter approached. I could handle fall but winter, now that was a different beast especially when the snow would come. Most of the time when Fat Boy had free time he would take me shopping or to the movies over on 125th Street in Harlem. That was our getaway from all of the bullshit. Everybody deserved a break and I know that we did. We had a lot on our young shoulders, more than we cared to admit, but we handled it the best we could.

"Alice, look, baby, I was thinking that I should confide in my moms about you. I'm not going to go into detail, I'll just tell her that you're in a "situation" and that me being your man and all that it is my responsibility to be there for you. And plus, with you being at the house would be a helpful thing because she'll have like a built-in-babysitter for Jada. Between my mom and her man and lazy ass babysitter having you around would be a benefit. It would save them some money because you'll be paying your room and board, food, electricity, and anything else that she might think of. I think I should confront her today and get it over with. The only thing she could say is no. We gotta do something, before you get spotted." I trusted Fat Boy with my heart and soul so I say okay.

It was a Wednesday morning; Fat Boy's mom had just stepped inside the house, on her way to her bedroom when he confronted her. I was peeping out of the door and eavesdropping to see how much time I had to split before things got ugly.

"Mornin' mom, listen, I need to talk to you real quick." Fat Boy said.

"Can't it wait, Marlon? I'm so tired," she said dragging her body to her bedroom door.

Fat Boy was persistent. He wasn't gonna wait any longer. "No, mom, it's a matter of life and death."

That got her attention real quick. "Come on in here, boy. What have you done now?" she said, as they entered her bedroom. I sat on the edge of his bed biting my nails down to the cuticles. I was on pins and needles not sure how this would work itself out. If she said no, then I was most definitely screwed. And if she said yes, then I had a lot of thinking to do because I knew that my stay wouldn't be forever. Nothing lasted forever. Nothing.

Fat Boy entered his bedroom with this strange look on his face. I knew that this was not a good thing, but then he broke out in a huge smile. A few seconds later there was a knock at his door, Fat Boy opened it and his mom was standing tall as a friggin' Amazon drenched in light skin and auburn curly hair staring directly into my face. I couldn't look her in the eyes. I just couldn't find the strength to do it but she managed to break the ice between us when she walked up to me and wrapped her solid arms around me. My head was buried in her lavender sweater that smelled like Downy mixed with Dove soap. God, she smelled so damn fresh.

"Hi, I'm Candy, Marlon's mom."

I looked into her hazel eyes and said, "I'm Alice. Nice to meet you."

She smiled.

I managed to crack a smile too.

Fat Boy told me that it was not an easy sell when it came to me staying with them. But like I said Fat Boy was a young man with the gift of gab. He managed to persuade her by having her look at how much money she would save. The fact that we were so young was a big concern of hers too, which I fully understood, but again, Fat Boy convinced her of how responsible I was for my age. My current situation was a prime example of that. How many girls did she know, at my age, who were homeless and not on the corners tricking to make a dollar to eat. At least she had to give me some credit. Fat Boy and I knew that her other concern was her man. It was bad enough that Fat Boy and his stepfather didn't get along, but she hoped that me being there would the ease the tension between the two of them. And her bringing up the fact that they would save money would be something her man would be delighted to hear.

The only time I left the house with Jada was if I had to go to the corner store. Well, one particular day, it was a Friday; I bumped into someone I never thought I'd see again. Egypt. Egypt nearly fainted in front of the bodega when she opened the door and Jada and I were exiting out. I literally had to catch her before she banged her head on the concrete. "Egypt, snap out of it! It's me, me, Alice."

Egypt was in complete shock. I had to ask the storeowner Miguel for a wet paper towel to dab her forehead with hoping she'd regain consciousness. I swear I thought we were going to have to call 911 and rush her to St. Joseph's Regional Medical Center. It took every bit of twenty minutes to bring Egypt back to reality. "Alice, what's wrong with her," Jada asked. "She's just not feeling well, that's all, don't worry, okay." I told her. She nodded her head up and down while licking on her cherry tootsie roll pop. Once Egypt came to, we talked and talked for hours while I let Jada play at the park. "Alice, I thought you were dead. That really hurt me to my heart. You and I were girls, you know what I'm sayin'." I nodded my head. "Why didn't you come to me?" she asked with sadness in her eyes. "I-I didn't want to get you involved. I didn't want to get anyone involved, but I had no one to call but Fat Boy. I didn't know what he was going to do once he saw me. I took a huge risk, Egypt." I said. I took at glance at my cell phone (that Fat Boy had bought me) and saw that it was getting close to noon, so I told Egypt that I would have to take Jada home for lunch. But before we left I confided in Egypt and told her where I was staying but I told her that I would have to ask Fat Boy if it was all right if she came to visit me. She was cool about it. Honestly, I didn't expect it to be any other way. Egypt was my girl.

When Fat Boy got home that evening I told him that I had bumped into Egypt at the bodega. I wasn't sure if he would be mad at me or not, but I still had to go to the store for Jada. I couldn't keep the child cooped up in the house all day long. He took a moment to think, and then he said, "I understand. You and Egypt go way back. Just be careful, Alice, don't mingle with too many people because everyone is not your friend. Niggas are grimy. Keep both eyes and ears open at all times." "I will," I said, then walked up to him and kissed him on his juicy lips.

Come Sunday, I got in touch with Egypt to come and

visit me. She did. I introduced her to Fat Boy's mom and stepfather. Fat Boy was out doing his hustle on the block with his crew. We talked and talked for hours upon hours. When his parents weren't home and when Jada was asleep we would smoke weed by his bedroom window. We would eat and watch stupid cartoons with Jada when she was up and running around like a damn lunatic high off of sugar. It was like old times.

One day, probably a Thursday, if I'm not mistaken, Egypt came over to visit me. It was near the end of February. Egypt had this sourpuss look upon her face. "What's wrong, E?" I asked her. "I'm gonna be leaving town." she said. "Why?" I asked her. "Girl, I met this pimp named "Graceful" and he's hooking me up with a gig at a Go-Go club. I'm going to be one of his dancers." I frowned. "Why are you going to do that?" "Look, Alice, you have Fat Boy and his family, people who care about you. I ain't got nobody. Mom's is still getting high. Half the time she doesn't know if I'm dead or alive. And she doesn't seem to care either. I need money, clothes, shoes, I gotta look out for myself." "But you're only thirteen, girl, what you know about being a stripper?" Egypt lowered her head in shame. "Don't knock me, aiight." She said. I sighed feeling bad for her. "I'm not. You didn't when I was doing my shit to eat. You kept it real with me, just like I'm doing with you. We girls, we look out for one another." "True that." Egypt said, with a smirk on her face. "I'm going to be traveling with him and his other girls. We're leaving tonight." My eyes got wide as saucers, "TONIGHT! Why you wait so long to tell me this shit?" I blacked out on her scrawny ass. Egypt shrugged her bony shoulders. "I didn't know how to break the news to you. Girl, you're in good hands." Egypt had a valid point, because I was in good hands. Egypt's eyes lit up. "Yeah, girl, I think I love him." She said with her head in the clouds. "And, girl, he loves me too. He said he gonna make me a star." "And you believe him?" I asked her. "I gotta trust somebody because I ain't got nobody else."

She said, and then cut her eyes down to the floor. I could see that she was getting choked up. Tears began to fall from her eyes and mine too. I think we smoked weed, cried, smoked weed, cried until it was time to say see yah girl.

***

Back at the Paterson precinct Captain Presley stood in his 7'1" frame coated in ivory-skin scratching his brunette mustache. He sipped on a cup of coffee while standing behind Detective Springs as he sat at his desk filling out paperwork. "'Ey Springs, any news on the double-homicide?" Detective Springs shook his head, "No, Captain, we haven't found the little girl yet. We have no witnesses either. There's no word on the streets about her either. It's like she vanished off the face of the earth. We know just about what we knew when this case first opened...nothing. Unless we find that girl, and find out what she knows, this case is going cold."

Captain Presley took another sip of his coffee, then patted Springs on his left shoulder, "She'll pop up sooner or later. Trust me, they always do. One way or another." He cuts his green eyes over at Springs, then walked back into his office and shut the door. Springs knew exactly what he meant by: one way or another—either dead or alive.

***

It was going into August. I was lying in bed when I heard this loud noise coming from Candy's bedroom. I tried to block it out by putting my hands over my ear, but it didn't help much. This was nothing new to me. Every time, Candy's boyfriend came home drunk he would stirrup a fight of some sort. I had a chance to get a good look at him. He stood about 5'11". He was caramel-complexioned with a receding hairline like George on the *Jefferson*. He had beady eyes, wide nose, full lips, and potbelly with big hands. I noticed his hands because of how huge they looked. He probably could knock the shit out of someone with one good punch with those bad boys. Another thing I noticed about him was that he didn't seem very friendly. If anything, he seemed like a disgruntle old man. Grumpy and always complaining about this or that like the world done him wrong, so he'd take his frustrations out on Candy. I know one thing he'd beat Candy like he hated her. Most of the time he would do it when Fat Boy wasn't home though. And every time he did Candy would never leak a word of it to her son. I think she was deathly afraid that Fat Boy would do something that he wouldn't be able to take back.

Just a week earlier, Fat Boy had pulled out a bat on him. "Try it, try it, motherfucker. Hit her again and I'll bust your head inside out. Nigga, I will kill you!" The fury in his eyes spoke that he was dead serious. He had had it with his mom getting beaten by his sorry ass. It was weird because even though his mom was the one getting her ass kicked on the regular, she would never cut his ass loose. It was baffling to me. I mean Candy didn't look her age, I guessed she was in her mid-forties, but she could easily pass for early thirties. She had a body to die for even after having two kids. She had long legs, pretty teeth, good hair that was hers. She had a good job working as a registered nurse in Hackensack, New Jersey. To me there was no reason for the mistreatment. But what I'd come to find out was that Candy, just like so many other women, including my mom around her age and even younger was afraid of being alone, so she settled for Bill thinking that that was the best she could possibly do. I begged to differ. She could've done so much better, if you asked me.

Here they were back at it again. Her screaming. Bill punching her likes a heavy bag. Her crying. Him shouting at the top of his lungs, threatening her that she ain't going nowhere. Her saying that she's calling the police, but never does. He'd dare for her to go ahead and call the damn cops, and if she does, he'll fuck her up for calling them. She'd start that damn crying some more, while asking him, why, why, do you do this to me—to us, huh? He'd laugh, while continuously whacking her with closed fists, she'd scream some more like he's damn near killing her. His words would slur, as he'd say she made him do it. Like it was her fuckin' fault that he was a lush. Like she said, go ahead and punch the living daylights outta me, nigga, maybe I'll grow to like it, and love you more for beating my ass. Then she'd start yelling again, no, no, it's the liquor, not me! Then he'd slap her across the face, WHACK, knocking her around the room likes a rag doll. Throwing her about the bed, against the wall, pushing her down on the floor, while choking her to death. After he'd given her two blackened eyes, then I'd hear them "knocking boots" like nothing ever happened. She'd start screaming his name and shit like that like he's fucking her so fuckin' good! Then she'd start crying again like a damn baby. It was just plain stupid. Stupid and ridiculous how they'd fight and end up fucking in the end. Was that what grown folks considered "foreplay" because if it was fuck that. I'd rather skip all of that and just get to the fucking.

Like I said they were back at it again. I couldn't wait for them to calm down. I never told Fat Boy about their frequent fights and fucking because he hated his ass. But he loved his mom to death. And he'd do anything to keep her safe, anything.

Earlier in the week Fat Boy told me that he had seen his ex-Nicole. He said that he told her that I was his girlfriend and that if she ever came back to his house that he would fuck her up. They exchanged words with her telling him that she would fuck me up on sight wherever she saw me. Promises, promises, I said. Well, it actually happened that Nicole and I did see each other. Fat Boy was in the bodega and I was outside smoking a cigarette (Newport 100s), when she approached me with her puppets, Angie and Crystal. They called themselves going to jump me. Well, we were about to do the damn thing when Fat Boy came out of the store and broke us up before things got outta hand. I had my Vaseline in my Gucci too. I was ready to whoop that bitch ass. She was going to take a beaten for everyone who had ever hurt me. I had no time to be getting into no shit especially with having the cops get involved. She threatened me. I threatened her. We left the scene and she and her gorillas took their asses on 'bout their business. I had been through too much *shit* to be letting something like a broken hearted chick scare me the fuck off.

***

One thousand miles away in Atlanta, Georgia…

"Honey, telephone, its Robert. Take the phone to daddy, Arionna." Arionna jumped up from the floor with her sister Angel and her brother Qwa ran to hand the phone to her dad. "Hey, Rob, wassup kuzzo?"

"What up, man. How's the family doing?"

"Everybody fine, just fine. Well can you talk man? I have something heavy to lay on you cuz." Robert said in his baritone voice.

"Lemme go in the other room for some privacy the kids are playing video games, here in the living room." Randy walked into their den and shut the door. He sat on the couch and put his feet up on the ottoman. "Wassup?"

"Randy, I know you and Leatravelle just bought a new house and the real estate business is treating you well." Robert said.

"Yeah, Rob," Randy, replied. "I'm finally living that

dream life I always dreamt of when we were young. I remember the pimping the drug dealing we used to do together, back in the days."

Robert interrupted his walk down memory lane. "Yeah, that's what I'm calling about, cuz. Remember Michele, Michele, the chick you had the baby girl with, man?"

"Yeah, man. I had to leave town, man. She was only 17 when I knocked her up."

"Yeah, cuz, well, check this out. I just found out that she was killed a year ago."

"WHAT! Wait a minute, what you talkin' about?" Randy asked, flustered. Then he quickly came to his senses. "A year ago! Paterson ain't but so big. You're just calling me about this now!" A grimace appeared on his face.

"Yeah, man, sorry, but I been busy, but yeah, she dead. Somebody blew half of her face off."

Randy couldn't believe his ears. He held the phone to his ear in silence. He was afraid to ask the next question. Robert broke the silence. "But Ran, check this shit out. They can't find your daughter, Alice. There are a million rumors going on here, man. Some say she was there when it all went down. Some say she got away. Some say she's probably dead and buried somewhere secluded. Some people say they've seen her. Some say nobodies seen her."

Robert and Randy stayed on the phone for thirty minutes. Robert informed him on what he knew about the murder of Michele. When they hung up, Randy just sat back motionless for what seemed like hours with tears running down his face. He couldn't stop thinking about the news he had just heard. His whole body was numb with disbelief and worry. Where is my daughter, he wondered?

A few minutes, his wife, Leatravelle walked into the den, she noticed how distraught Randy was. "Honey, is everything all right," she asked with a concerned look on her dark-skinned face. She sat her 5'5" body next to him on the couch. She noticed his eyes were watery and red like he had been crying. She touched his shoulder and then massaged his broad back. "Do you want to talk about it?" Randy pondered over the thought of sharing his past with his wife of ten years. He had never told her about his daughter, he never felt the need to, but now things were different. It was then that he realized how much Alice really meant to him. So he turned and look his wife in her chocolate-brown eyes, took a deep breath, and began to share the horrific story of how a woman he once knew was dead and how the daughter they conceived together was now missing.

Leatravelle remained silent the whole time Randy spoke. It was a shock to her, but she remained faithful to the man she'd fallen in love with. Randy had already made up his mind that if she went ballistic the fact of the matter was that Alice was his biological daughter and no matter how his wife felt he was going to do everything possible to find her, whether dead or alive. The only question that parted from Leatravelle thin lips was, "Randy, how old is she now?" Randy took a moment to think, "Well, she gotta be at least 13 or 14 by now," he said, "The last time I saw them she was 6. Michele had thrown me out of her house and told me to never come to see them again." He lowered his head and massaged his face, vigorously. "Listen, I have no secrets. I was young and so was she. It was a different me, back then. I don't know why I never told you, Lea. Maybe I just wanted to block out the pain, but I love my daughter. Always have, always will."

Leatravelle nodded her head as if she could relate to what her husband had stated. She knew all too well that sometimes your past could come back to haunt you. The only thing she could do, as she's always done, was to continue to stand by his side through thick and thin.

"I often thought about Alice. Wondered how she was doing, if she missed me or hated me, you know." Randy said, his voice getting hoarse.

Again Leatravelle remained silent. She was the type of woman that came from a family of strong women. She knew what it was like to have an absent father. She was a confident, smart, and independent woman. Leatravelle often reminded Randy of Michele, when he first met her at the coffee house. She was gorgeous, witty, and down-to-earth. She was just a real wholesome woman. That was the connection that bonded them all of those years. But he wondered what had gone wrong with Michele for her to get killed. What changed? There were so many questions running through his head. He couldn't think straight.

Randy stood to his feet, "I don't understand, Lea. Michele never smoked. Okay, she got pregnant young, had Alice, her parents got killed in a car accident, but she managed to keep a job and go to college. What changed?"

Leatravelle stood and walked toward Randy standing by the wall unit. "Listen, I know that you are your own man. That's whom I fell in love with. I don't care about who you used to be, because as you've said you are a different person now. As far as Michele is concerned, you being separated from their lives, you don't know what they've endured. Anything could've happened to changed things. You just don't know, and being an estranged father too, left Alice in a vulnerable place. Wherever she is she is probably scared, alone, and feeling abandoned. *We* need to find her."

Randy turned around and looked his wife in her eyes and remained silent trying to hold back the tears that were flooding in his eyes. The only words he could find to say was, "Thank you, Lea, for being so supportive. Woman I don't know how I'd function without you. I love you, baby."

She wrapped her solid arms around him and gave him a big bear hug. "I love you, too."

***

Egypt had come back to town after she had been on the road for several months with her pimp, Graceful. It was her birthday weekend in September, when she had gotten in touch with me. I was still living with Fat Boy chilling with my two new friends, Shay and Mecca. Shay was twelve but she had a body on her. She had thick jet-black hair, big titties, and ass for days. She stood about 4'11" with deep-dark skin, but her best assets were her eyes. They were big, brown and beautiful. Mecca was short, chubby, with shoulder-length ash-brown hair. She had a big gap between her two front teeth as well as her legs. She was high yellow. Word on the streets was that she was quiet but a hot ass for eleven.

Anyway, we were laughing and joking, just having a good ole time. I invited Egypt over to hang out with us. Within twenty minutes, Egypt was ringing my doorbell. As soon as I opened the door I grabbed her and gave her a big hug. I was so excited to see her and hear all the juicy gossip about being a stripper. We had so much catching up to do.

"Girl, get in here." I practically pulled her in the house. Shay and Mecca were sitting on the couch in the living room. Jada was asleep. Candy was at work as well as her boyfriend. Fat Boy was with his crew.

As soon as Egypt walked inside the house, I introduced Egypt to my girls. "Shay, this is Egypt, Egypt, Shay. Mecca, Egypt, Egypt, Mecca." Everybody seemed to click, which was cool. "Let's go into my bedroom," I said. Egypt sat down on the edge of the bed dressed in her fly gear. Mecca and Shay sat on the floor Indian style. And I sat on this milk crate that Fat Boy had by the window. "Where'd you get those boots from, girlllll. Those joints is hot!" Shay asked. "Oh, a friend bought them for me." Egypt said, winking her eye at me. I knew the scoop. "Graceful" had bought them and anything else she owned.

"Listen, I heard some rumors." I said. "But we can talk

about that later."

"Nah. It's cool. I ain't got shit to hide." Egypt said. Shay and Mecca was all ears.

"Well, word on the streets was that Graceful was kicking your ass. Heard you got beaten pretty badly. I heard he was known for beating his bitches and forcing them to have sex with him."

Egypt interjected, as she felt being put on the spot, "Nah. He's not *that* bad. Every now and then, everybody gets their ass kicked. If he didn't care, he wouldn't…"

I had a grimace on my face. *Is she for real*, I thought to myself? "Girl, that's not love. Fat Boy never put his hand on me. Egypt, you my girl still and all, but c'mon, that shit ain't fly."

Feeling like the center of attention, Egypt changed the subject. "Look, at this ring he bought me, girlllll!"

"He ain't bought you shit, you the one dancing for that money." I told her.

"60/40 for your information…*don't* you see these clothes I got on. Look at my UGG boots, girl." Egypt boasted like she was top shit.

"But you ain't got no money in your pocket," I said, knocking that ghetto bitch back down to size.

"It's my birthday, girl, I don't need no money. You bitches are treating me all day to whatever I want. And you's can start now, let's go down to the liquor store, I'm thirsty. I'm drinking Grey Goose, tonight on you guys." Egypt pursed her lips like her shit didn't stink.

"We can't cop nothin' to drink." Mecca and I said in unison.

Egypt seemed to have all the answers, "Alice, you and Shay can get in. Ya'll look older than us. Shay looks like she's 18. And *you*, Alice, you can easily pass for 20 tops. C'mon let's go."

As soon as we were about to head out the bedroom, I heard Fat Boy's stepfather yelling at his mother in front of the door. They were at it again. Fighting like cats and dogs. I can't tell you how embarrassed I was, but Shay, Mecca, and Egypt all seemed to understand.

I decided to call Fat Boy to let him know that I was going to the store.

"Hello."

The yelling grew louder and louder through the door.

"I'm going to the store with my girls."

"Ok, just be safe."

Before I hung up, Fat Boy said, "What's all that noise I hear in the background?"

"Your stepfather and mom. He's drunk again, baby."

"Ok. I'm coming home. I'm tired of that motherfucker messin' wit' my moms."

"FAT…" I tried to respond, but he hung up too quickly.

Damn, I said to myself. *I should've never even called him*, I thought to myself.

Finally, the yelling simmered down in the hallway. They seemed to have gone back into their bedroom. I was so glad Jada was at her grandmother's house.

Shay was eavesdropping by the door, "Sounds like they're away from the door," she said in a whisper.

"Ok. The coast is clear," I said, as we hurried out, down the stairs, and out the front door.

"Damn, you can hear Fat Boy's stepfather yelling all the way out here," Mecca said, while cutting her eyes up to the window.

"I'm use to it," I said, as we were walking down the street. "One minute they're yelling, next minute their fucking, and then he is snoring fast asleep."

"That's what the cheap gin will do to your ass." Shay said.

"He drinks that NottyHead," I said.

All of us started laughing. "Show us how you dance on the pole, Egypt," Shay asked her.

Egypt dropped it like it was hot. She tried to make her booty clap. We all busted out laughing because she didn't know how to do it right. She was too stiff. She looked so funny. We laughed as we were walking down to the corner.

"At least, I'm using what I got to get what I want." Egypt exclaimed.

Mecca had something on her mind so she set it free, "Egypt, if you got so much buy this damn drink yourself!"

Egypt rotated her neck, put all of her weight on one side, and rolled her eyes, "Like I said before, it's my birthday! I ain't buying shit!"

As they were walking into the liquor store, Egypt smacked me on the butt. I turned around with this crazy look on my face, "Girl, I know you ain't turn lesbian on me. Look, I'm strictly dickly."

"Me, too," Shay and Mecca said simultaneously, as they walked in behind us, laughing out loud.

In the store, we all walked around like we were looking for something, while Shay went to the register to pay for the Grey Goose. As I turned to walk down the second aisle, I completely froze. My mind drifted back to the house, in my bedroom, as these two guys were walking toward me, one I remembered so vividly. He was the one in my bedroom, I thought to myself. Instantly I started shaking in my shoes, hoping he didn't recognize me. Fear was written in my eyes and all over my face. Don't remember me; don't remember me, I kept repeating in my head. He cut his eyes over at me for what seemed like a split second, dropped his head, while the other guy looked at him and then cut his eyes over at me trying to figure out what was going on.

"Yo, man, you know her?" The other guy asked him.

"Nah." He replied, as they both walked passed me.

I dashed out of the store.

***

Smoke turned his head to the left, then right as he looked

at Sincere with perplexity in his eyes. "What you looking at, nigga." Sincere said.

"Yo' why that bitch was lookin' at you like that?" Smoke asked.

"Whatchu mean?" Sincere asked.

"C'mon, man. You know what I'm talkin' about."

"Nah, man, I don't." Sincere said as he waved his right hand at Smoke. .

"Why the fuck did she looked at you like she knew you, huh?" Smoke said. "Ain't that the crackhead bitch we killed daughter?"

"You crazy, Smoke. A young bitch looks at me and you gotta blow things outta proportion. Why you trippin' all of a sudden, huh?"

Smoke paced back and forth in front of the liquor store. "I dunno. I dunno. Something just don't feel right to me, you know?" Smoke repeated over and over and over again.

All the while Sincere had to figure out a way to distract Smoke before he realized that he didn't fulfill his obligations of killing everyone, including the girl in the house that day.

"Man, we drinkin' or what?" Sincere nonchalantly asked, hoping to distract Smoke's train of thought. "Yeah, I'm drinkin'." Smoke replied, still with a bewildered look upon his face as he reached in his front pocket and pulled out his wallet and slipped out a crisp twenty-dollar bill and handed it to Sincere. "Yo get whatever." Smoke said still deep in thought. Smoke kept looking up and down the street. Sincere wasn't sure what would come of him not completing the job as Big Ray had commanded. He was nervous, but he couldn't very well show any signs of edginess to Smoke because if he did, he knew he was a dead man walking. *That black dress that Big Ray often talked about would become a reality for my mother.* And that thought alone kept Sincere walking on eggshells.

***

I was huffing and puffing, looking back, over my shoulders as I sped walked down Market Street. It took Egypt, Shay, and Mecca a minute to catch-up with me.

"Hold up, girl." Egypt yelled.

"What's wrong wit' you? What's wrong? What happened?" Shay asked.

"You look like you saw a ghost," Mecca exclaimed.

I tried to get myself together, but Mecca hit the nail on the head when she said that I saw ghost. "Nothing, I'm ok. I have to go to the bathroom that's why I'm speed walking." All three of them frowned as if they knew that I was playing them out like they just got off the yellow bus or something. I didn't want to scare them and I didn't want them to panic either. My life was on the line and felt like the end was near if he caved and told his friend that it was me, why didn't he, I wondered? It had to be a reason —one that I would probably never know the answer to.

As we were turning the corner on Beech Street, bright lights blinded our vision. Mad cops were everywhere. Patrol cars were blocking the street so that no one could come in or get out. It was crazy. "Alice, looks like the cops are at Fat Boy's house." Egypt pointed out. There were spectators scattered like ants wondering what was going on. I started running toward the house, but a tall white officer restrained me. "I live here. I live here, mister," I said repeatedly with tears engulfing in my eyes. I just knew something bad had happened. "What's your name?" The same officer asked. I had to think quickly on my feet. "Donna...Donna. I'm the babysitter. What happened? What happened, officer?" I asked in a crackling voice. "Aren't you a little young to be watching someone's child," he said with a peculiar look on his oatmeal-colored face. "I look younger than I am. Blame it on my mom." I nearly broke down trying to crack a smile.

God, it hurt to bring her up. But I had to think of something and quick.

Before he got a chance to answer my question, there were two other officers, both on each side of him, one tall and one short hauling Fat Boy out of the house in handcuffs. They were holding him like he was a dangerous animal. Tears released from my eyes. My heart was pounding in my chest. I could barely catch my breath. At the same time Fat Boy's crew were running down the street as the officers were putting him in the backseat of one of the patrol cars. Everybody froze and stood in disbelief. One of the cops, a short, stout Hispanic guy came out with a pair of creamed-colored latex gloves on as he carried out a clear plastic bag with a .45 caliber in it. Candy was on her knees with her hands behind her head crying her eyes out. She had blood drooling down her face and arms. She was shaken up and disoriented. I wasn't sure if she had been shot too, but I figured if she had they would've rushed her to the hospital. Bill must've beat the shit outta her. Candy screamed so loudly, as Jada was crying and kicking her feet at the air as another officer, tall, deep-dark-skinned man carried her away. Jada was stretching her little arms out with big tears pouring from her doe-eyes wailing as her screams shrieked and snot ran profusely down her little nose begging earnestly for Candy to come and rescue her. "MOMMY! MOMMY! MOMMY! MOMMY, DON'T LET THEM TAKE ME! MOMMMMY!!!!!! MOMMY! MOMMY! Please!!!! HELP MEEEEEE!!!" There was such terror in her eyes. Jada threw a fuckin' tantrum. And I couldn't very well blame her. Her whole world was being shattered in one fast swoop. I felt so sorry for her. God, the pain I heard in her voice left me numb. A few minutes after that two medium build white men came out of the house dressed in dark navy-blue uniforms with purple latex gloves on carrying a black body bag on a gurney. They hauled the body into the back of a black van. Got in and drove off.

Immediately I knew that it was Bill in that body bag. I

just knew it. My knees felt weak as I fell to the ground with my mouth dangling open, no words came out, but tears were leaking from my eyes. It seemed so surreal. I couldn't believe this was going down. Egypt, Shay and Mecca stood motionless. They were in tears too. They didn't know what to do to comfort me. They tried to lift me up off the ground, but I was like deadweight. It was complete and utter chaos.

I was hearing bits and pieces of the story of what had occurred at the house, but I'd come to find out that no one on the outside really knew what went down but Fat Boy, Candy, and unfortunately dead Bill.

***

Why'd he have to hit my mom, Fat Boy thought to himself sitting in the back seat of the patrol car. The sirens were bellowing above his thoughts. He flinched when he heard the gun pop in his head. All he had to do was leave. Walk away and come back with a fresh state of mind, but no, he couldn't be the bigger person and now Bill's dead, he thought. A flashback of what had occurred at the house rewind and fast-forwarded in his mind as the officer zoomed through the winding streets of Paterson with red lights swirling and sirens echoing throughout the neighborhoods to the precinct on Broadway.

Bill was on top of mom, choking her in their bedroom. In a split second I ran in, ran to my bedroom and opened my closet and reached up on top for my silver box that housed my .45. I ran back in mom's bedroom, didn't ask any questions, and fired two shot...POW! POW! One bullet hit Bill in the back of the head. The other bullet hit him in the back. I heard sirens rushing in. At first, I wouldn't let the cops in, which forced them to call this a hostage situation. I heard a lot of commotion outside as I peeked out of my mom's window. I quickly gave myself up when my mom told me to. I didn't want to. What about my girl, Alice, I thought. Before turning myself in, I turned to my mom as she sat shivering on the floor with tears and snot running from her nose. "Mom, please, please, if I turn myself in, don't you make Alice get out. Promise me. Promise me, that you'll let her stay for as long as she needs to." Mom quivered as she nodded her head up and down, barely able get her words out, "I will, son. I promise. Please, don't make this worse than what it already is. Please, Marlon, please, turn yourself in. I don't wanna have to bury my child, please, please," she begged. It literally ripped my heart out of my chest to see her cry. I hated to see my mom cry. But mostly, I hated to see her settle for an ass kicking to keep a fuckin' low-life. When was she gonna realize that she deserved so much more, I wondered.

Fat Boy came to.

He was taken to a juvenile detention center and booked for first-degree murder. He wasn't released in the custody of his mom either. The judge ordered him to be contained until they decided whether to charge him as a juvenile or adult. They wouldn't even let Alice see him. Fat Boy wondered what would come of Alice. She'd been through hell and back and now this. All he could hope for was that something good came out of something so bad. *How is Candy going to be able to afford me a lawyer? I pray she doesn't get me a public defender, because if she does, I'm a goner. They will fry my ass. I'll never see the light of day again*, he thought to himself. He didn't know if Alice knew how much she meant to him. He loved her with every vessel in his being. He also hoped that her feelings didn't change toward him.

***

I knew with everything in me that Fat Boy truly loved me. No. There was no doubt in my mind. For him to be fifteen, he showed me what love truly meant. And I felt so blessed to have met him. So blessed.

I knew in my heart that this was not going to get any easier. Things seemed to get harder and more unpleasant. I felt so alone. I mean, my mom was dead, my dad was nowhere to be found, Fat Boy was locked up, and my reality really slapped me hard in the face. I completely understood how Egypt felt. Yeah, it was real, and it hurt like hell to be caught up in all of this mayhem. I had no one to turn to. There was no one to trust. No one. I was truly on my own. I lay sprawled across Fat Boy's bed smelling his body scent from the sheets and pillowcase. I cried feeling so empty inside. I missed him so much. It felt like my heart was being torn from my body. Yeah, that's how much it hurt. It seemed everyone I loved, left me by the hands of destruction. Knowing that I was alone I had to figure out my next move. I mean I couldn't stay at Fat Boy's house forever. Someone was bound to snitch on me. It had gotten to the point where I started to feel like I couldn't trust my girls. Yeah, I was paranoid. And I had good reason to be; this was a matter of life and death... mine.

***

When Sincere dropped Smoke off at his house over on Marion Street they didn't say two words to one another. Smoke seemed deep in thought, trying to put two and two together about the girl. He remembered sending Sincere upstairs to check and see if anyone else was in the house.

He also remembered Sincere stating that he wouldn't shoot a kid. His mind was racing with so many thoughts. Racing a 100 mph until he gained a throbbing migraine. The sharp pains in his temples didn't stop him from trying to figure out what might've occurred. Within less than twenty minutes, Smoke snapped his finger I got it! He said to himself, while lying back on his bed with one arm propped as a pillow. *That nigga must've saw that girl in the room*, he thought. *He didn't kill her!* His eyes grew dark as he raised his body from his bed, picked up his cell phone and called Big Rayvon, but he kept getting his voicemail. He called Big Ray's driver Driff's number and got through. "Yo, this is Smoke, lemme speak to Big."

"Big Ray is out of town on business." Driff said in his deep baritone voice.

"How long will he be gone?" Smoke asked.

"Two weeks."

"Damn! This is fucked up, man!" Smoke snapped.

"You wanna leave a message? I'll make sure he gets it first thing."

Smoke mellowed out. "Nah. It's cool. I'll wait until he gets back. Thanks, anyway. Bye."

Smoke pressed the "end" button on his cell phone and stared at the floor for what seemed like hours trying to figure out why Sincere played him like that. Didn't he realize that not fulfilling the obligations of what Big Ray had requested would cost them both their lives? Did he even care? Or was he looking out just for self and that bitch fuckin' daughter? His head was pounding so bad that he laid back and closed his eyes to block the madness out because deep down he knew that it would only get worse. He had the gut instinct that it was just a matter of time before Big Ray got word. And once that happened someone was going to catch a beat down or bullet.

***

Sincere sat in his Lexus with his engine off on a side street near Pennington Park, on edge and heavily in deep thought. His first thought was to flee town and visit some family in Baltimore. But he wasn't the type of nigga to run from nothing—not even a bullet. Damn, fuck, shit! Spewed out of his mouth as he popped the steering wheel, hard, cracking a couple of knuckles. He'd rather stay in Paterson and suffer the consequences of his actions than to run and have Big Ray harm his mom. His mom was his pride and joy. He would take a bullet for her—and only her. Sincere couldn't believe that he bumped into that girl, and of all places here in Paterson. Why, why, why, he said over and over again. Damn, and why did Smoke of all people have to be with him? Sincere's mind cluttered with thoughts of what might happen to him. The last thing he wanted was for anyone in his family to get hurt. He was at a crossroad and the outcome of this was anyone's guess. *I wonder if Smoke will tell Big Ray*, he thought. He tried to block that thought out of his head, but he just couldn't so he came to the conclusion of, fuck it, whatever happens, happens. He made up his mind to wait and see what Smoke would do and how he acted around him. If he was fidgety and shit he knew that something bad was about to go down. His main objective was to keep both eyes and ears open. Any day could potentially be his last. He hoped this wouldn't lead to anything between him and Smoke. Smoke was his main man but Smoke also had a dark side to him. His greed would cross any nigga regardless if they were *boys* are not. When it came to money, Smoke would off anybody, including him. He cut his eyes out the driver's side window, *I won't hesitate one second or hurting Smoke if he comes at me sideways*, he thought.

***

After one week it was evident that I would have to leave Fat Boy's house. Candy started buggin'. Taking her anger out on me. Candy went to visit Fat Boy two times following the week of the shooting. Unfortunately I couldn't go because I wasn't his immediate family. But in 7 days, I had written him 7 letters professing how much I loved him and how sorry I was for everything that had happened. I took part to blame because if I had not told him, possibly none of this would've happened. I remember he wrote on one of the letters: "Baby, it was bound to happen sooner or later. Don't go blaming yourself. I lost my cool." It made me feel good that he took accountability for his own actions.

In the last letter, I also told him that I was leaving his mom's house. I didn't go into detail because I didn't want to cause any confusion between the two of them. They needed each other in the worst way. I needed and wanted him too, but I had to think about myself. I promised him that I would stay in touch as much as possible, and that I would also remain his girl through thick and thin, that I would always stand by his side until the end. All I could hope was that he believed me.

One day I overhead Candy talking to a public defender named Mr. T.M Myles. Some white dude from some hick town who decided he wanted to come to the ghetto and represent a thug. That was some bullshit. Mr. Myles looked like a nerd—straight up nerd. To me, it was a setup to put Fat Boy away for life. I overheard Candy saying something about how they were going to try Fat Boy as an adult. I know Fat Boy had to be pissed that she couldn't afford an attorney. I shook my head from side to side, numb. It hurt me to my heart to hear that. You just don't know how bad it made me feel. Obviously the prosecutor didn't buy the whole self-defense story. I think that if Candy had reported the domestic abuse they might've had a better case, but Bill always seemed to persuade her not to by hitting those soft spots and making her forget that he had just whooped her ass. Man, he must've had some good ass dick to make her all of a sudden have amnesia. They also didn't buy the fact that Fat Boy was coming to his mother's aid by trying to protect her. How he feared that Bill might've killed her had he not intervened. Fat Boy didn't stand a chance once they proved that Bill was unarmed with his back to Fat Boy.

Anyway, Mr. Myles promised Candy that he would do his best to get a lesser charge. I prayed that that was true. God, I prayed. I remembered back when Fat Boy recited the Lord's Prayer to me. Well, it came in handy this particular day. No doubt.

"First degree is never gonna standup in court," Candy repeated his words verbatim. "And *your* gonna prove that he was trying to save my life," she confirmed, while nodding her head.

After they hung up, Candy sat at the kitchen table thinking, *the first real man who showed me love was gone. Gone.* She lowered her head and began to weep, silently.

I was having a difficult time swallowing all of this. I continuously blamed myself. If only, became my favorite words. If only, I didn't call him none of this would've happened. If only, I stayed in the house. Deep down I believed that Candy blamed me for Fat Boy's actions. She didn't have to say it directly to my face. Her actions spoke louder than her words. She tried to be cordial toward me but it seemed so fake and phony. It wasn't sincere as when I first came to her home. Candy was a nervous wreck and it affected her in so many ways. She stopped going to work. She stopped taking care of herself. She stopped eating. She had a difficult time sleeping. She suffered from insomnia. Most of the time she'd be up at the crack of dawn sitting in the living room seemingly in a daze. Dried tear streaks were on her grief-stricken face. She looked like death was walking over her. Candy was losing herself and it really hurt me to watch her fall so low. Yeah, it hit me hard so I had no choice but to leave before Candy did something that she'd regret and something that I could not live with. Yeah, I feared that she might try to commit suicide. You had to be there to see what I saw for me to come to that conclusion. She loved her son with heart and soul. Yeah, it was that evident. And so did I, so therefore, I felt the need to part from her sight so that maybe she could get herself together and try to restore what was left of her life.

I grabbed my satchel and the rest of my belongings, as I daydreamed about the past last year. Before stepping out of the bedroom I remembered to get my picture that was hidden underneath the mattress. The picture was all crumpled even though I had it wrapped in plastic wrap. I seemed stuck in a trance, while staring at the picture, when I heard a car horn blow. Yeah. So much had happened since meeting Fat Boy. I had just mailed him a letter, but I didn't dare tell him what my plans were. I figured I'd let Candy do the honors.

I exited out of the house, didn't bother to leave a note behind for Candy. She'd know that I was gone. Outside there was a white Cadillac waiting in front of the house with the engine running. In the front seat were Egypt and her pimp Graceful waiting patiently for me. My back was against the wall so I had no choice but to reach out to her and her pimp. Yeah, I guessed you could say that I was falling too. For me to stoop to this low and decide to sell myself and give Go-Go dancing a try. I knew Graceful was a no good nigga, but I didn't have too many options and no one to turn to. I knew that the cops could still be looking for me. So I made my mind up to make enough money to get the hell out of Jersey and start a new life elsewhere. I'd send for Fat Boy and we'd live happily ever after. Yeah, I was dreaming, so what. Everyone deserved to at least dream, right?

I hopped in the backseat with a look of distress on my face. Egypt took the liberty of introducing us. "*Daddy*, this is Alice." Graceful turned around and looked me dead in my eyes. "Sooo you want to join my family," he asked me in his husky voice. "Yes," I said. I don't know what the fuck Egypt saw in that dude. I mean…damn was he big as hell! He was fat, black and dressed in a Steve Harvey suit. Pinstripes were not becoming of him at all. "Well, if you not full of shit or lazy you can make plenty of money. Do you know how to dance?" Before I could respond, Egypt cut in, "Hell yeah! She…" Graceful snapped his finger and gave Egypt a look that said shut the fuck up, bitch, I was talkin' to her. Egypt immediately stopped talkin'. "Well, I have certain rules that must be obeyed. You work six days a week. I get all the money and I give you your cut every Friday." I interjected, "But Egypt said it was 60/40." I said with a distraught look upon my face. "Really, well, I guess we can talk about that later," Graceful said with a sly grin on his ugly ass face, as he slowly drove off like he had a fan club or something. God, he made me sick!

Graceful thought that he was the shit like he was some big time celebrity and everyone should be honored to be in his presence. I thought he was full of shit. *Damn, how did my life get so fuckin' complicated*, I thought to myself.

As we arrived at Graceful's bachelor pad, Egypt showed me her bedroom. She was livin' large. She had mad shit. A walk-in closet full of designer clothes, racks and racks of shoes, a slew of designer bags: Prada, Burberry, Fendi, and Vuitton. Girlfriend was not fabricating a thing. I was a bit jealous, I will admit. Her bedroom looked like that dude Nate Berkus came to her house. I mean it was off the hook. She had a big ass sleigh bed with mahogany headboard, leather loveseat, a nice throw rug that looked like it cost some money, big screen TV, nice CD/DVD player. She had a CD rack filled with every rap artist you could think of. Yeah, she had it all and then some.

"C'mere, Alice."

I walked over to Egypt as she was gazing out of her

bedroom window. "You think you will like it here?" she asked. My eyes lit up like high beams. I looked at her like she had three heads. "What! Are you serious, this place is the bomb." I said excitedly. "Keep it real with me, Egypt…what do you do to get all of this?"

"Dance, I told you. I just dance that's all," Egypt said confidently.

"C'mon E, be real. I mean I ain't tryna play you out but it gotta be more goin' on than just dancing. Look around. Look at where you are and where you've been. And plus, you ain't that good of a dancer, so what gives, girl." I chuckled and nudged her in her side.

Egypt sucked her teeth and lifted her middle finger up at me, and then she walked over to her loveseat and sat down. I remained standing while gazing out at the beautiful landscape. God, it looked like paradise to someone like me. Fuckin' paradise.

I walked over to the plush red loveseat and sat beside Egypt.

"Listen," Egypt said, "*Daddy* is not easy to please."

"I kinda figured that out." I told Egypt.

"Yeah, well, I gotta get you ready. Daddy wants his girls to be top notch, no mistakes."

I nodded my head. "Well, let's do the damn thing then." I said with mad confidence, but deep down I was shitting bricks.

Egypt's eyes scrolled me from feet to face. "First, I need to take your measurements. Get you some fly gear. Makeup. I don't know if you are into wearing a wig or just your real hair, but its good to be dramatic. Men like that. They like to fantasize." She said. Egypt was schooling me like she was a pro. It wasn't like I had just gotten off the yellow bus or nothing like that but this dancing shit was a new thing, new gig to make some quick money, that's all.

As we were talking someone knocked on Egypt's bedroom door. Egypt rose to her feet to answer it. It was Graceful. He entered her room like he was this giant of a man. He stared at me, hard, like he was looking through me. I can't say that I wasn't a bit intimidated by him, because suddenly I was. It was something about his stature that diminished me bit by bit. His aura was like poison to me. Yeah. Poison.

"You ready." Graceful asked me, staring at my crotch area. I felt so naked standing before him. Butt naked. "Yes, Daddy, she ready." Egypt said, "Daddy, I told her everything that is expected of her." I nodded my head. Graceful continued to gaze at me with this strange look in his eyes. I felt chills run up and down my spine. Yeah, Graceful gave me the creeps.

"We gotta get your fake ID. How old are you anyway?" Graceful asked me. "Thirteen." I said. He nodded his head up and down and pulled on his salt-n-peppered beard. "Well, you look like you could pass for twenty-one, maybe twenty-two tops. You're stacked nice. Nigga gonna love your big ass tits, that round apple-shaped ass, thick thighs and wide hips. A nigga a pay top dollar for you, I have a way of knowing these things. It must've been something in that milk you were drinking. Anyway, listen, anything you need to know or if any situation happens to come up and you don't know how to handle it, ask Egypt. Since Egypt's stage name is Fire, I'ma name you Desire. Fire and Desire, hot damn! It's perfect." Graceful said excitedly, then he got serious and that stern looked appeared on his face. "We leaving in an hour so get her ready." Graceful did a once over of me and then swaggered out the door.

I closed my eyes and took a deep breath asking myself, girl, what have you just gotten yourself into.

I felt so strange being onstage with eyes gawking at me. Even though I had on this sexy getup, I felt naked as a jaybird. I mean all of my goods were exposed. Men were trying to touch me, while rubbing their crotch areas. They were lusting, but in a bad way. It made me feel sleazy, dirty like I was doing something so beneath me. I heard Egypt say, "Relax," as she was dancing along side of me to get me warmed up before she let me go solo. "Feel the music, girl. Feel the music!" Egypt said as she was feeling on her tits, and maneuvering her hands down to her pussy, and then working her hands back up to her tits and making them kiss. Then she started undressing herself, piece by piece, until she was damn near naked. I had to take my mind off of her before I fucked myself. I mean this was another side of Egypt that I was not used to. She had definitely changed and I couldn't say if it was for the better.

This white man with brunette hair dressed in a business suit was sitting at the bar; I mostly focused on him because I found him to be attractive. He looked clean—rich clean. He had a lot of money in his hands. He crumpled up a twenty-dollar bill and tossed it at me and asked me to show him my ass. "That's right, brown sugar, let me see that black ass of yours." He said in a raspy tone. I started make believing I was on HBO, on one of those porn flicks and I started emulating their movements, moans, and acting like I was this nasty bitch. The more I did naughty things the more money he tossed onstage. By the end of the night I had about one hundred dollars, but I knew that that money would be going in Graceful hands, not mine. That part sucked. I was doing all the work and that black muthafucker was making all the loot. What kinda shit was that! Yeah. It was fucked up!

Egypt got offstage and sat next to this chocolate-colored dude at the bar. He was making eyes at her all night. He already had a drink waiting for her. I guess they knew each other, well; it was obvious that they did. His hands were like ants all over her body. And she didn't seem to mind one bit that they were out in public. Actually, no one did. I thought she said this was strictly dancing, I said to myself. Yeah. Dancing, aiight, but it looked more like trickin' to me.

As I was doin' the damn thing for white man I noticed he was touching himself. I could tell that I was getting him hard by the look on his face. He was beating his dick and he made it seem like it felt so damn good to him. I tried to distract myself by moving to the other side of the stage and as I danced in this slow droppin' it like its hot motion, this other white dude had his eyes on me too. I felt like both white dudes were in competition for me to pleasure them. And I was doin' it too.

The music was pumping with "Taste Like Candy" by Cameo, where I could really get into it. I started showing off my moves, twirling my body around in a seductive motion, lifting my arms up and slowly bringing them down, sensually, gliding my wet tongue across my lips, smiling with my eyes and making them dreamy like, caressing my ass, feeling on my thighs, tits, and pulling at my nipples and sticking out my tongue in a slutty way like I was about to cum onstage. I had those fools drooling at the mouth, while jerking their dicks. Them hands kept flinging their crumpled money onstage, and I kept dancing until I drained their wallets, pockets, and dicks dry.

Once I felt confident enough I gave this one black guy a lap dance. I was massaging his hard dick with my ass as his hands groped at my body. I closed my eyes and pretended that I was sexing Fat Boy. My head tilted back, lips parted, I moaned, as I felt myself cream between my legs. The man was licking on my neck, earlobe, and yanking on my tits. I moaned louder playing along as if we were actually fucking. I let him have his way by letting him slip his finger in my thong and swiping it between my fleshy folds. My pussy was sloppy moist. That muthafucker got so horny. Next thing, I knew his bouncer body was shuddering and his eyes were rolling in the back of his head like he was having convulsions. While this was going on, my mind drifted to Graceful. Is he going to make me start turning tricks or maybe sleep with him, I wondered? All I was interested in was dancing, nothing else. Just dancing. I had hoped that Graceful wouldn't make me do things against my will. I promised myself that the best thing for me to do was to stay out of his way. I'd dance and give him the money. He'd give me my cut and I'd stash it away to get me as far away from Graceful, as possible. I thought about Fat Boy too. I mean I wanted to be able to send him money whenever he needed it. And now that I had that fake ID, the thought of going to see him crept in my head too. I told myself, the first chance I get I was going to see my man.

***

For the last two weeks, Smoke had avoided Sincere. Sincere was all but sure Smoke would tell Big Ray when he got back in town. And that he did. He didn't leave anything out either.

"The night at Michele house…" Smoke said, "Yeah, the girl looked spooked when she saw us at the liquor store…" Smoke continued, "I'm almost 100% sure the little girl was in the house that night. I'd bet my life on it."

Big Ray sat on the couch dressed in his gray suit with burgundy stripes taking in everything Smoke had told him. "Well, if this is true, we have a big problem. Ok. If I need you can you handle my problem, Smoke?" Big Ray asked.

Smoke didn't hesitate to respond. "Yeah, what they say, you brought him in, you have to take him out. Yeah, I got you, Big."

"Okay, lemme talk to Sincere first. Have you seen him lately?"

"Nah. Not since that night."

"Okay, I want you to treat him like nothings wrong." Big Ray said.

"Aiight. I got you."

"But listen, Smoke, if I call you and say: Go walk the dog, then you handle it."

"Got you, Big, no problem."

As Smoke exited out of Big Ray's office, he realized that he really didn't want to hurt Sincere. But he also didn't want to spend the rest of his life in prison either. With the girl seeing Sincere's faces she could very well ID him. Smoke told himself over and over that he had no other alternative. Sincere fucked up! Smoke knew that if he handled this properly that he would gain major points from Big Ray. Big Ray was like a father figure to him and he wanted to make his father proud.

***

Two months had past. I was becoming a real moneymaker. I was making a name for myself, well, *Desire* was. Some of the girls were beginning to get jealous. Some of Graceful's top girls were getting jealous too. Everyone wanted to book the two sexiest dancers: Fire and Desire. Look, this was an equal opportunity so if they wanted to keep up with me they had better put their game faces on. I was on a mission. Get paid. Get out. Get my own.

Graceful was acting a little different towards me. Was I going to be his main woman? Honestly, I couldn't tell if that was what he was thinking or not. But I can tell you that it didn't cross my mind. Not one bit.

"Desire, c'mere." Graceful said directly me with his index finger. I loved the name Desire because it made me feel like a different person. I could forget about Alice when I was Desire, all the pain—the neglect, all the confusion…everything. It was all in the past when I transformed into her.

I was sexy and well liked. The name gave me a certain presence and attitude.

"What's up, Daddy?" I asked while strutting over to the bed where he was sitting sipping on a glass of orange juice.

"C'mere. Have a seat next to me," he said patting the bed with his massive left hand.

I sat down.

"Listen baby," he said, "It's about time you stepped your game up a notch."

I thought I was, I thought to myself.

"I think you got what it takes to be a star. You're young, beautiful and you got class and sex appeal. Baby, I'm in your corner 100%. We're going to be around some high rollers tonight and this weekend. If somebody offers you the right price, I want you to do a date, ok."

I sighed. "*Daddy*, I really just want to dance. I ain't with all that extra stuff. I make just as much or more than your other girls who turn dates, so why do I have to fuck if I'm bringing you good money?"

"Because no money is enough money. Sex is mental, baby. It's like you're there but not. I was there for you, right? Now I need you to be there for me. I got big plans for you, Desire. Big plans..." he nodded his head and massaged his silky palms like he was up to no good.

***

"Hello?" Smoke said when he answered his cell phone. The manly voice on the other end said, "Go walk the dog." Click.

Damn, Smoke said to himself. Damn, fuck, damn! Sincere, fuck! Smoke was beginning to bug. He knew what he had to do. And he wasted no time. He pressed the ten-digits on his phone.

"Khalif, this is Smoke. Where you at, nigga?" The two of them spoke for about fives minutes. "Meet me in thirty minutes at the spot," he said. Khalif knew where the spot was. Obviously he had done this before. They hung up, and Smoke started pacing the living room floor in his one-bedroom apartment. He felt a little apprehensive about what was about to go down, but he had a job to do. He had to make Big Ray proud. That meant something to him. He was glad that him and Sincere were chilling again. Things weren't quite the same between them, they had many falling outs, but they were still dawgs.

Smoke didn't hesitate to call Sincere. "What's good with you, Sin?"

"Nothing much. Just watching some TV." Sincere said eyes glued to the Lakers game.

"You still gonna put me on that spot where I can have a radio put in my BMW. You know I got to get some sounds in my new ride." Smoke chuckled.

Sincere turned the volume to the TV down. "Yeah, man, I got you. Them kids are in there all night putting systems in." Sincere told him.

"Cool. Then I'll scoop you up in like two hours."

"Okay, I'll be ready, homey. Peace, one." They hung up.

In the last two months, Sincere figured all was well. He knew if Smoke told Big Ray he would've been dead by now. He also knew, Big Ray wouldn't send Smoke to do his dirty work. He'd hire a hit man first. Someone he didn't know and who didn't know him—someone with no conscience, no worries, no cares—someone ruthless and conniving. Smoke and him had known each other since second grade. And they had also been out a few times recently. To him, Smoke was like a brother he always wanted but never had.

Sincere leaned back in his wife beater T and plaid pajama bottoms and lit a blunt. He watched some more TV since he had time to kill. It was already 6:00 p.m. He figured he'd take a shower and start getting ready around 7:30 p.m., to hookup with his boy.

Smoke called Khalif back and they spoke for about

five minutes and hung up again. The plan was set. In two hours, something horrific was about to go down and Sincere was none the wiser.

***

Fat Boy was sitting in his cell, staring down at the floor. He lifted his head up and looked over at his cellmate, Saabs squatting in the corner like he was taking a shit. Saabs was writing in his notepad. He was big on spiritualism and whatnot. His tall, dark muscular frame was no stranger to prison. He had been locked up since he was twelve years old. *Something ain't right, something just ain't right. Even though this jail is so far, my woman's letters are starting to fall off,* Fat Boy thought. *I only saw her once, when they had me at the County, and then she couldn't look at me straight. Nah*, he shook his head from side to side, *something ain't right with her.*

His cellmate, Saabs must've read his mind 'cause he said, "Man, didn't anyone ever tell you when you in jail you don't got no woman? What part of that don't you understand? Now you can sit over there stressing about something you can't control or you can sit back and do your time with a clear mind. Don't let time do you, son. You ain't been here six months yet and you done had about five fights. I'm tellin' you Fat Boy, don't do it to yourself. Now your girl probably loves you and all don't get me wrong, but now she has to think and do for herself. Some women handle it better than others. Some women get one nigga to fuck until they man come home. Some run around fucking every Reggie, Robert, and Ron, you feel me? Only you know what kinda woman you got. And what I mean by that is you know where she came from and where she's been. Son, you can't turn a ho into a housewife, but a housewife can turn into a ho. Now I don't know your lady, but I can bet you one thing, she

132

ain't sitting around waiting to die. So start living man. Your body is locked up but not your mind. So stop letting your mind run wild. Control your mind, Fat's."

Fat Boy sat still taking all of his boy's philosophy in.

***

Smoke pulled up to Sincere's house. He blew his horn, twice. Sincere was already dressed in his shaggy jeans and oversized sweatshirt with Tims. He was putting his gun in the backside of his pants. He took his gun out maybe five or six times, indecisive on what he should do. *Nah, we just going to the radio shop*, he thought. But deep in the back of his mind he said to himself, fuck it, and slipped his gun back in the backside of his pants, and headed out the door.

The music was blasting when Sincere opened the passenger side door. "What up, man." Sincere said as he sat down in the soft leather and stretched out his long legs. Smoke's head was bopping to DMX CD, It's Dark and Hell Is Hot, track 7, "Get At Me Dog" and then he switched back to track 6, to replay "Fuckin' wit'd", as he drove off. He could see why Smoke needed another system. It was loud, but he needed more volume.

Smoke was smoking some weed and passed it over to Sincere. "So how much you think I got to spend on this system, man, to get a nice one in here?"

"It's gonna be about $500.00. But your shit gonna be right. They hooked me up, and you heard my system." Sincere said taking another hit of the weed before passing it back to Smoke. They rode for about ten minutes and then Smoke said, "Yo' Sin, can I ask you something?" "Yeah," Sincere replied. "When we went to those crackheads house and killed them, was anyone else in the house?" Sincere sat up straight. He had this eerie feeling come over him. His heart started beating fast as hell. He played his anxiety off nicely, "Nah," calm, cool, and collected. He showed no signs of guilt, none whatsoever. "Why you asking me this now, Smoke?" "Because the little girl was looking at you crazy in the store that day. And I figured why else would she react that way." Smoke said annoyed. Before Sincere had a chance to respond, Smoke said, "Oh shit! Oh shit! Ain't that Khalif over there?" Smoke pulled over. Sincere already knew that Khalif was bad news around the 'hood. "Why you gonna stop for that nigga," Sincere asked him. "Damn, nigga, it looks like his car broke down. Why you trippin'?" Smoke pulled up side-by-side Khalif's Audi. "What's up, Khalif?" Smoke said. "My shit ran out of gas, Smoke. Can you drop me off at the gas station? I can take a cab back. I'll pay you, man." Sincere cut him off before Smoke could respond, "We in a hurry, man. We tryna catch the radio spot before it closes." Smoke jumped in the conversation, and cut his eyes over at Sincere, "C'mon, man, I'll drop you off at the gas station. There's one right down the street from the radio spot." Smoke turned his head toward Sincere, "You know the gas station I'm talkin' about, right, Sincere?" Sincere gave Smoke a funny look as if to say, what the fuck! "Man, hop in." Smoke told Khalif.

Khalif hopped his 257-pound, dark-skinned, lazy eye self in the backseat, as Smoke drove off.

"Well," Smoke turned to Sincere, "was she there?"

"Who? Was who there?" Sincere said.

"The little girl. Was she in the house that day?"

"Why you talkin' about this shit now, Smoke?"

"Some shit just don't make sense. You should've killed her, Sin." Smoke said, as his eyes grew dark. "You should've killed her." He nodded his head in the rearview mirror as if to give the okay to Khalif to handle his business. Sincere looked over at Smoke realizing that he was being setup. Sincere quickly leaned forward and reached for his gun, but he was a second too late. Khalif gun was already pointed at the back of his head. Khalif pulled the trigger without a second thought…a loud echo ringed in the car. POW! Sincere's head and body fell forward on the dashboard with blood spewing out everywhere. "Damn, that shit blew half of his head off," Khalif said with a smirk on his chubby face. "Where you gonna dump the body?" he asked Smoke.

"Down by the river, under the bridge." Smoke said, as if he planned this slaying precisely.

They stopped at a secluded area in the industrial area of Bunker Hill and wrapped Sincere in a blue tarp and stuffed his body in a black plastic bag, and then they waited until it got darker and dumped the body in the murky Passaic River.

"Let's go get my shit washed." Smoke said.

They both got back into the car, Khalif sat in the backseat, lit some weed, took a long pull, as they drove off blasting DMX, "Niggaz Done Started Something."

***

Graceful stood over me, as I sat on his king-sized bed pointing his long finger in my face. "Desire, I thought I told you I wanted you to start doing dates!" he snapped, his spit landing on my forehead. I stood up in my peach teddy; "I don't see why I have to sell my *pussy* if I make my quota for you every night I bust my ass on that stage dancing." Graceful drew his right arm back, high above his head, then he came down with severe force, SLAP! I fell backwards against the wall. The other ladies were sitting in the living room; they heard the thud and jumped up. One of his women, Rekindle spoke up. "*Daddy*, want some pussy?" Whenever that nigga start whipping on your ass he was ready to fuck. Another woman of his named Provocative said with her country ass, "Gurl, and the crazy thang is the ass whipping is longer than the fuck."

135

All ladies laughed except Fire. Fire took it personal. "Bitch, you love to get your ass kicked. You love when Daddy chokes you and slaps your ass, and calls you dirty names before he fucks you. You told me that shit the other day, bitch." Fire had this don't-give-a-fuck-about-you-bitch, look on her face. All the ladies broke out laughing again because they were happy it wasn't them. Sometimes his beatings could be fatal where you had to be admitted in the hospital. Graceful had a bad temper and the girls knew how far to push him, but I was new to the game. I was still wiping the Similac off of my mouth as far as Graceful was concerned.

Back in the bedroom, Graceful picked me up by the neck and slammed me hard against the wall again. He threw me down on the floor; on the way down I hit my head on the corner of the footboard. I fell to the floor. Graceful picked me up and laid me on the bed, and he ripped off my teddy and climbed his big ass on top of me and raped me while I was fading in and out of consciousness. His left hand cupping my neck like a crab's claw, as he slapped me hard with his right hand, I saw stars. My body started shaking like an epileptic.

Graceful was still inside of my warm tunnel, pumping his dick deeper and deeper in me as he was sweating bullets, beads of sweat dripping off of his forehead onto my breasts. He was fucking me like he hadn't fucked in years. He pressed his full, thick dark lips against my left ear. God, I could feel his hot breath evaporating in my skin.

"Now, listen, bitch, you gonna fuck me and whoever I want, wherever I want you to. Do you understand me, bitch?" I tried to nod my head but I had a terrible headache. "Yeah, yeah, I understand, Daddy." I replied feeling nauseous.

"You gonna learn about respect, bitch. Just like the white man taught us niggers, you gonna learn who the fuckin' master is, bitch. You understand me? I can't hear you, bitch." My mouth was watery but I managed to get the words out that Graceful wanted to hear. "Yes, Daddy, I understand."

Graceful then let me up, kissed me on the cheek, and smacked me on the ass. "Now go get cleaned up. Tonight is a special night. I got some important people coming through. I need you to look your best. And I got another secret for you. If you keep working and making money like you been doing, I'm gonna make you my main lady. My Bottom Woman in charge of all these bitches."

I stood feeling wobbly. My legs felt like weak links. My head was pounding and my pussy was throbbing with pain, not pleasure. I walked out of his bedroom with my right hand pressed against my pounding head. I just wanted to lie down, lie down and cry my heart out. I wanted to fall asleep. But my mind wandered wondering how Fat Boy was doing. I was using a guy named Jayson, from the bar address to write him. He wasn't nobody to me, just another nigga sweating me to give him some pussy.

Anyway, when Fat Boy replied to my letters I would get them from Jayson. The last time I heard from Fat Boy he said that they were going to sentence him as an adult. He wouldn't tell me how much time that meant, but I knew it would be a lot.

***

"Can the defendant, please, rise?" Judge Redden, a white blonde-haired man with brown eyes who looked to be in his latter forties spoke in his baritone voice. Fat Boy stood to his feet dressed in a dark grayish jumpsuit chained and shackled. "You have been found guilty by a juror of your peers. These are unusual circumstances surrounding this case. And even though you're being sentenced as an adult, I'll take it all in consideration. But all in all there still was a crime committed. Someone died by the hands of another. A life was taken with an unlicensed weapon. So I must still follow the guidelines and the law. I have read all the letters sent in by your family and friends. And I have read every motion filed by your attorney, and I can honestly say that no one wins today. But I hope everyone surrounded in this case has learned that domestic violence and illegal weapons have no place in our society. We have a couple of statements to be read by the victim's family members."

One by one, each family member approached the podium to read their profound words.

"He was a good man…who didn't deserve to die so heinously…" one dark-skinned woman said.

"I miss my uncle Bill already…" the young light-skinned girl said in a crackling voice.

One woman could hardly speak, as she ran out of the courtroom.

Then Fat Boy's mother, Candy made her way up to the podium to speak on her son's behalf. She wondered why no one spoke about Bill's drinking problem or how he beat on women. After she finished her statements judge Redden spoke.

Fat Boy stood to his feet again looking the judge dead in his eyes. Judge Redden asked if he'd like to say anything to the family.

"No, your honor." Fat Boy replied.

The roar of the crowd echoed.

"ORDER! ORDER IN MY COURTROOM." Judge Redden banged his gavel, repeatedly. "ORDER! Let me remind you all that this is a courtroom. I will not tolerate any outbursts from the courtroom when the sentence is read. Marlon Brown, you are here by sentenced by the Superior Court of New Jersey to 15 years to life."

Candy screamed so loudly it could've awakened the dead. She fell back and fainted on the floor. The courtroom became chaotic.

"ORDER! ORDER IN THIS COURTROOM." Judge

Redden banged his gavel, repeatedly again.

Fat Boy turned and took one last look at his mom lying on the floor, passed out. The court officers grabbed him by the forearm. "Mom! MOM!" His eyes spread wide. "I'm just trying to see how my mom is doing, muthafucker!" He tussled with them, all the while yelling as his voice chanted like bells along the walls and high ceiling. "I'm just trying to see how she's doing! I need to make sure she is all right. Mom! Mom!" Fat Boy yelled at the top of his lungs, "Mommmmmmmmmmmmmmm!!"

"Remove the prisoner from this courtroom," Judge Redden commanded.

The two officers dragged Fat Boy. "Don't worry Marlon, I'll file an appeal." Mr. Myles said as he kneeled to Candy's side, awaiting the paramedics. It was too much for her to stomach. She was losing more and more of herself and that day pretty much emptied her out. She was beyond restoration. Her fragile heart could only take but so much more anguish before she completely surrendered and gave up.

Candy came to before the paramedics arrived. They checked her for observation anyway. Mr. Myles left her side to get her a bottle of spring water. The paramedics helped her to her feet. "I'm okay," she told them. "I just need some fresh air," she said, while heading out to the lobby of the building. Mr. Myles swiftly walked behind her. "Ms. Brown, I promise you the sentence will be overturned. I assure you this would never hold. This will never stand under appeal."

"15 years, 15 years…he was just trying to save my life. Please, Mr. Myles, please, help my son," she pleaded with tears running fast down her face. She then walked off with her head dangling low as her knee-length skirt swayed in the summery breeze.

***

As soon as Detective Springs looked at the bodies with the other detectives, police officers, he spoke out loud. "Well, here goes another setback in my case, huh?" Springs had been looking for the culprits of this heinous crime for months now. One of his street informants named Grudge, a short, brown-skinned man probably in his late fifties told him that somebody by the name of Sincere, another young cat might have had something to do with that double-murder that happened a while ago. Springs hoped that if he could find Sincere he might get a lead in the case. Now he was back to square one, but he was optimistic that something would fall through the cracks and help him solve this case. He often thought about the missing girl, so hopeful that he'd find her before it was too late.

Benny's cell phone rang.

"Come meet me over on at the bridge by the Blue Lagoon. We have something you need to see." Detective Springs told his partner.

"I'm on my way."

Detective Benny arrived within ten minutes. The area was blocked off by yellow tape. Several police officers were at the scene. A black van was there too.

Detective Benny exited out of his car, dressed in his makeshift business suit, and headed toward his partner Springs.

"What do we have here?"

"A decomposed body. Looks like he's been floating for at least three weeks. A young man walking across the bridge noticed his body and frantically called the police." Detective Benny pointed to a seventeen-year boy standing by his patrol car. "Said he was coming from basketball practice. I got his name and address just in case."

"Good. Any ID found on the body?" Detective Benny asked Springs as they were walking toward the black van.

"Nada. He just had clothes on his back and the Timberlands on his feet. We won't know anything until after they do the autopsy."

Detective Springs sighed, scratched his scalp, while staring into space for a brief moment. "Check the area for shell casing, anything, okay."

Detective Benny nodded his head.

"Get everyone down here ASAP. Call me if you find anything. I mean anything, Benny." Detective Springs demanded as he walked back to his patrol car, bewildered and frustrated. He wondered if this had anything to do with the Banks case, but he had no clues to compare the two. That agitated him even more. I gotta figure this shit out, he said to himself. I'm going to solve this case, if it's the last thing that I do, he promised himself.

When he got in his patrol car, he lit his cigar and leaned back in his seat and took a long pull off of his cigar. With his right hand he lifted the small Styrofoam cup of cold coffee out of the cup holder that he had sitting there since early that morning and took a sip, and then tossed it out the window, and sped off with an ominous feeling in his gut.

***

Three years later…

I was sixteen. And Egypt was fifteen, but she looked much older from dealing with drugs. Graceful held us captive all those years. Other girls came and went, but he refused to turn us loose. Some stayed at their own will for like months, others for days at a time. I noticed a kind of resentment from Egypt. No. We weren't as close as when I first got into the game. I was now Graceful's "Bottom Woman" and I guessed Egypt felt played and betrayed. She was deeply in love with Graceful, but I don't think he realized it or he simply dismissed it from his mind. I was handling more of his business affairs. I gained his trust and started collecting his money. I drove his Cadillac to drop and pick the ladies up from the Go-Go bars. And no, I didn't have a driver's license so I had to be extra careful when I was driving. I made sure I looked older and acted the same. Most of the time the cops never paid me any mind, which I found to be strange since they were supposedly looking for me. I was right under their nose, and they didn't even know it. I didn't have to work as much. And I stayed home and worked side-by-side Graceful. When all the other ladies had to work their asses off to make that money to fill Graceful's pockets. All the things Egypt did, I was doing for him. So I could understand why she despised me so much. I was not taking her man but I could understand how it might've looked that way. I had to stay on Graceful's good side to stop him from beating me senselessly. I needed him to confide in me so that I could know his every move. I wasn't doing this for kicks. I was doing it to stay alert and alive. Egypt just had to find it somewhere within herself to understand that, but I figured that wasn't going to happen because she was in waist deep as it was.

"How come she's taking my spot, *Daddy*?" Egypt asked with her arms crossed about her chest.

"You must've forgotten who the fuck I am, bitch! And who you are fuckin' talkin' to." Graceful snarled at her, then he mellowed out as he cut his eyes over at me sitting at his desk counting his fortune. "Now if you must know, Alice has been having fainting spells. I can't have her dancing and falling the fuck out onstage, now can I? It wouldn't be good for business."

Egypt couldn't stand to hear anymore of his lies so she excused herself, but I could tell that she was furious. She rolled her eyes and sucked her teeth. That's some bullshit, she mumbled as she was exiting out of the family room. Egypt wasn't bold enough to say how she truly felt directly to Graceful's face because she knew that could cost her an ass kicking. None of the girls in the house was ever bold enough to defy him and think they'd live to tell about it. Egypt studied Graceful's pattern to a tee. She knew him more than she knew herself or me. It was like she was obsessed with him or something. She knew that I made more money than she did even with me not dancing. Even still, she felt that she should've been Graceful's #1 "Bottom Woman" because she put me on. Egypt felt she had earned the title Bottom Hoe and who was I to come in and disrupt her happiness. It was pretty fucked up, I know. She introduced me to the game, showed me the ropes, and schooled me on the Go-Go industry. She was there for me when I had no one else. After Fat Boy had gotten locked up, Egypt came and got me. If it weren't for her, God only knows where I'd be. I could've been in jail or homeless or dead. It wasn't like I didn't care about Egypt's feelings because I did. And my plan was to make things right between us but I needed just a little more time, but I felt like time was surely running out for me. I didn't know why but my gut was telling me that something dreacful was about to happen. *And* I knew that I was going to be caught in the middle assed out.

***

Wassup Fat Boy,

I hope you're aiight in there. Listen, I got some bad news to tell you. It's bad enough you're locked up. You don't know what's going on on the outside so I'm about to tell you about your so-called girlfriend, Alice.

First of all, the bitch ain't shit! Out here trickin' for this pimp named Graceful. Alice is his top hoe. Selling "your" pussy to every fuckin' nigga she can get. I know its foul, man? After all you've done for her, how she gonna play you for a fool. She's sucking all types of men's dicks too. And she's dancing at the Palace Playmates Go-Go Bar over on Rockland Ave. She goes by the name Desire. She's been dancing for 3½ years now. All of a sudden, the bitch is having fainting spells. Sometimes she can be so melodramatic. I know Graceful can get beside himself. He likes to beat his bitches down. He pounced Alice around from time to time. Banged her head on the footboard, one time too. After that the migraines started, so she says. Fainting spells started too, although, she hasn't had a seizure as of yet.

I know she had you thinking that she was working at the mall for the past few years. Well, now you know the truth. That skanky bitch don't love you. You don't need her. My advice to you is to cut that bitch loose and do you.

Look, I know you ain't got nothing but time, but at least you won't be wasting your thoughts on that bitch-ass hoe.

Hope all is good.

Peace, my nigga

Egypt smirked, and then stuck out her long tongue and licked the seal of the envelope. She then addressed it to:

Marlon Brown #1234567
Mid State Correctional Facility
Wrightstown, New Jersey 12345

Egypt affixed a stamp to the envelope with no name or return address. She slipped it in the side compartment of her Coach bag until it was time for her to go to work. She figured she'd ask Jayson from the bar to drop it in the mailbox for her. Jayson owed her a favor, especially after she had given him some of her juicy pussy for free the other night. Of course, Graceful was preoccupied entertaining his lady friends so he was oblivious, but she was well aware that if he'd ever found out her ass was as good as dead.

Egypt was shrewd in knowing that once she exposed Alice her relationship with Fat Boy would disintegrate and her heart would be crushed. Egypt knew how much Fat Boy adored Alice. How much he loved her too. She knew that an ultimatum would be enforced. Alice would only have two choices in order to remain his girl: stop dancing and leave Grace or forget about him. There was no in-between when it came to Fat Boy. He had a one-track mind and nothing was going to sway his decision.

Egypt knew Alice's heart too. She knew that Fat Boy meant the world to her. She knew that Alice had written him frequently and sent him money too. The prison Fat Boy was in seemed a million miles away so she barely had a chance to go visit him as much as she would've liked. It was impossible to sneak away from Graceful for that many hours. All of this animosity erupted because Egypt felt that Alice was strongly stealing her limelight and she was pissed. She was Graceful's "Bottom Hoe" long before Alice came along and she'd be damned if she was going to be dissed because of some amateur two-bit hoe.

In her mind, Alice needed to be dismissed from her, Graceful, and Fat Boy's memory. She wanted her to be a forgotten thought, a once-upon-a-time misstep that had exited out of their lives.

***

A week had gone by. I was sprawled across my bed, crying hysterically in my goose down pillow. Someone had knocked on my door, but I never welcomed them to come in. They knocked again. Still, I never responded. I guessed they heard me sobbing. After the third knock, Egypt walked in in her striped nightshirt with bare feet and big rollers in her hair.

"You aiight?" Egypt asked.

I wiped my wet face with the back of my right hand and turned over on my back dressed in red boy shorts and a black T-shirt that read: #1 Chick. My voice cracked when I spoke, and I was hoarse too. "No. I just got back from visiting Fat Boy."

"Is everything okay?" Egypt asked, with a look of jubilance hidden behind the composed look that was plastered all over her devious looking face.

I tried to calm myself down, but it was much too painful for me to do so. I stuttered to get my words out. "He-he-he…" I could barely speak without breaking down, crying louder and louder until I was a puddle of wounded sobs. "He-he-he told me to never write him or come back to see him again. He gave me a choice: stop dancing and leave Graceful alone or forget about him." I told her.

"Damn! Girl, whatchu gonna do?" Egypt asked as she sat on the edge of the bed.

"I dunno E. Dancing is all I know. I don't have my high school diploma or GED. I can't get no other job that's gonna pay me like this one does. I dunno what to do, to be honest." I sighed deeply feeling the hurt splitting inside of me. "Fat Boy told me if he ever saw Graceful, he would kill him. I believe him too. You should've seen his face, the pain in it, especially his eyes. He was crying, girl. Then he stood up and walked away from me. He wouldn't tell me how he found out or nothing. He knew everything, Egypt, everything! It had to be one of the other bitches in the house who ratted me out." I cried even harder placing my wounded face in my damp palms as I wondered, how could they have known about Fat Boy? How could they have known that I was *his* girl? Nothing was making sense to me but I knew someone was trying to breakup my happy home that I had hidden deep inside of my heart.

Egypt rubbed my back trying to console me. Egypt had an eerie look in her eyes and a grimace on her face like she was suddenly pissed the fuck off. "This shit is fucked up, Alice!" Egypt's voice snapped as if to bite off someone's head. Slowly the softness in her tone and eyes recovered showing empathy to me.

"But whatchu gonna do? Whatchu gonna do, Alice?"

I shook my head, baffled. "I dunno." I replied, with red and weary eyes and a ruptured heart that once was as solid as a rock.

***

Fat Boy paced back and forth in his cell with fury buried in his eyes. He couldn't keep still, to save his life. He didn't eat, barely slept since Alice's last visit. His stomach was full of butterflies. One minute he was scratching his stomach, then his balls. Then the next minute, he was rubbing his head, then his eyes. He was stressed to the max. He kept getting headaches that lasted for most of the day. He couldn't seem to get a grip on things. Alice had him pretty fucked up inside and out.

Fat Boy was so angry that he was looking for trouble. He wanted to take his frustrations out on someone, anyone, just to get the hurt out of his system. His cellmate, Saabs tried to stay out of his way. He was so afraid of the way Fat Boy was behaving that he didn't say much. He never told Fat Boy that he knew Graceful from out in the streets. Nope. Saabs never peeped one word.

In the past, Graceful had brought girls to dance for him and his boys' several times when he was a free man. Saabs figured it would be better to not tell Fat Boy of this valuable information. He didn't want to be the cause of any mishaps. Saabs wanted to remain a prisoner of peace and spirituality. He didn't need any negativity floating around him, not even in prison. It took him years and years to become the man that he was today and he wasn't letting anyone stunt his growth or mental peace. Those days were long behind him and he wanted to keep it that way. To him, some things were better left unsaid. And this was one of them.

Saabs also knew that Fat Boy didn't know that even though Graceful was a pimp, that he was also a very dangerous and malicious man. Graceful knew people and was very popular. He was known to hurt men, women, anyone who fucked with his money and his bitches.

"Fat Boy, get a hold of yourself." Saabs said while lying on the bottom bunk.

Fat Boy kept pacing back and forth. "Nigga, if you know what's best for you, you will leave me the fuck alone." He stepped toward the upper bunk and retrieved the letter from underneath the thin mattress. He unfolded it and began to read the letter again and again and again and again and again quietly to his heart and thoughts, as he continued to pace the concrete floor back and forth with temples throbbing and agony in his eyes.

Wassup Fat Boy,

I hope you're aiight in there. Listen, I got some bad news to tell you. It's bad enough you're locked up. You don't know what's going on on the outside so I'm about to tell you about your so-called girlfriend, Alice.

First of all, the bitch ain't shit! Out here trickin' for this pimp named Graceful. Alice is his top hoe. Selling "your" pussy to every fuckin' nigga she can get. I know its foul, man? After all you've done for her, how she gonna play you for a fool. She's sucking all types of men's dicks too. And she's dancing at the Palace Playmates Go-Go Bar over on Rockland Ave. She goes by the name Desire. She's been dancing for 3½ years now. All of a sudden, the bitch is having fainting spells. Sometimes she can be so melodramatic. I know Graceful can get beside himself. He likes to beat his bitches down. He pounced Alice around from time to time. Banged her head on the footboard, one time too. After that the migraines started, so she says.

Fainting spells started too, although she hasn't had a seizure as of yet.

I know she had you thinking that she was working at the mall for the past few years. Well, now you know the truth. That skanky bitch don't love you. You don't need her. My advice to you is to cut that bitch loose and do you.

Look, I know you ain't got nothing but time, but at least you won't be wasting your thoughts on that bitch-ass hoe.

Hope all is good.

Peace, my nigga

After the fifth read Fat Boy wondered who mailed him the letter and why. The thought of sharing the letter with Saabs had crossed his mind but it was too close for comfort. Too personal. Too emotional. And too painful. He didn't know whom to trust anymore. For all he knew, Saabs could've been the culprit fuckin' with his head for his own personal amusement.

***

"Somebody call 911! Call 911!" Egypt's voice shrilled from the stage of Palace Playmates Go-Go Bar. The blonde-haired pale-skin barmaid quickly called. "We need an ambulance! One of the dancers collapsed onstage. Yes. 735 Rockland Ave. Please hurry!"

"Call Graceful, Rekindle." Egypt told one of her girls.

"Hell no!" Rekindle replied, "she's going to the hospital this time."

All the girls knew that I kept having those fainting spells and all Graceful would do was wait until I woke up to take me home. But then he'd have me right back in the bars the next night. It was no dark secret that the fainting began after the beating and me hitting my head on the footboard.

The paramedics arrived and rushed me to St. Joseph's Regional Medical Center, here in Paterson. This white nurse with crimson hair and pale skin subtly approached me while I was lying in Bed #6 in the emergency room.

"How long have you been having these fainting spells, ah, Ms. Banks?" she asked me.

My head felt like someone had hit me over the head with a hammer. I squinted my eyes, "About 3 years or so."

The nurse's eyes widened, "Three years and you never had your head examined?"

I slowly shook my head no.

"Well, we are going to have to run some tests on you. The doctor will see you and he may requests you to have a CT scan done. So just relax yourself, okay. Oh, your sister is outside on the phone. She couldn't get a signal on her cell phone in here. She'll probably be back in a few minutes."

At first, I looked at her with perplexed eyes but then it hit me that maybe one of the girls had told her that they were related to me. I slowly nodded my head to respond. I tried to talk minimally because the pain was so tormenting. God, it hurt to even breathe.

I had been in the hospital for a week. Dr. Hyatt, a tall, white, blue-eyed blonde-haired man stood by my bedside and explained the findings of an aneurysm in the back of my head. I remember him telling me that people have lived their whole lives with one as long as they took their medicine and saw their doctor on a regular basis that I would be all right.

By Monday, I was being discharged. The same nurse with crimson hair filled out all of my papers and explained everything to me in great detail. "Remember to take it easy, Alice. No bumping of your head into walls, young lady." We both laughed. I must admit it was kind of funny the way she said it and all.

The nurse continued, "Make sure you get your medicine right away. And remember to keep your doctor's appointments, I can't stress that enough, okay."

I nodded my head.

Even though I hated the hospital with a passion, I enjoyed my 7 days stay because I needed to rest my body, as well as my mind. I wasn't too concerned about the hospital bill because I had a fake ID, and any and all information I'd given them was bogus.

As the nurse wheeled me out to the lobby entrance to wait for Graceful's Cadillac to pull-up, so many thoughts raced through my head. I knew that soon my dancing career and relationship with Graceful would come to a screeching halt. I just didn't know exactly when it would happen.

Suddenly my mind drifted to Fat Boy. God, I missed him. I still loved him so much. Here I was turning 18 in a couple of months. I had been working for Graceful since age 13. For five years of my life I dedicated to him, and it was the most painful five years of my life.

Now knowing that I had the aneurysm I knew that I would have to slow down tremendously. Yeah, I knew that but I wondered how Graceful would react. I always wondered what and how he would react to certain things because of his greed for money. He didn't care about others. It was about him and only him. And that bothered me a lot.

As I was getting dressed I thought about my life before all of this mayhem. Before Steve came into my mom's life. Before the Dempsey's. Before Fred. Before my mom's murder. Before Candy and Bill. Before all the pain began, my life was good. I had my mom and she had me. I also thought about my nanny Angelita, how she was my guardian angel. I wondered how Angelita was doing and if she was in a good place in her life. Back then Mom and I were happy. My dad, Randy seldom crept in my head. After so many years of neglect I realized that it was up to him to be apart of my life. I had no idea of his whereabouts but I often wondered if he knew about mines.

Months had gone by. September was here and so was my 18th birthday. Graceful was being generous by giving all of his girls that night off. Rekindle, Provocative, Fire, Cradle, Drizzle, and me. Graceful also had this pimp named Jada Million at the house with his entourage of hoes. Jada Million was a thin fellah who had facial features of a rat. I swear, he looked just like one with the beady little eyes and all. He wasn't an attractive man by far but he had money coming out of both of his holes. He'd shit and cum money simultaneously that's how bad that muthafucker was. Jada Million was known for sporting fedora hats and loud colored suits and Stacy Adams on his feet with his signature cherry flavored chew stick gripped between his teeth. He was flashy with his clothes and car. Driving around in an outdated bright ass yellow Cadillac Eldorado with whitewall tires. The chicks he brought with him were considered his baddest bitches, but to me they were more like "busted bitches". All of 'em had bullet hole bodies, they were skinny as rails, had dark spots on their skin, and glued hair weaves with the tracks showing, cheap clothes and Footprint shoes. C'mon, they definitely were no competition for us. Graceful always made sure we were dressed to the nines. He had a reputation to uphold and we had to represent.

Anyway, all three ladies accompanied the rest of us in the living room. We were smoking weed, drinking, and dancing. Well, they were smoking weed and dancing. I was sitting down sipping on a glass of Chardonnay taking it easy.

Graceful and Jada Million were in his bedroom conducting business bagging up some cocaine as well as sniffing. Even though Graceful was a pimp himself he sold coke too. He knew with it being his #1 ladies birthday it would be a lot of other pimps, hos, and hustlers coming over who indulged in cocaine too.

The CD player was blasting song after song. The ladies were stoned.

Within about one hour, there was a knock at the door. I rose to answer it since I was the closest to the door. People starting to come already, I thought to myself. I mean it was early. I peeped out of the peephole to see who it was. It was two female boosters Cameo and Queeney, I knew. They often came over to sell the girls clothes and cosmetics.

"Hey Desire, Happy Birthday!" They said excitedly.

"Thank you," I said with a huge smile on my face.

I noticed that Cameo and Queeney weren't alone this visit. They had this clean-shaven man with them. As they walked in, he swaggered in too dressed in black from head to toe. And he smelled so damn good I wanted to eat him up.

"Oh, this is a friend of ours, Desire. He's cool."

"Hello." I said to him.

"Happy Birthday, Desire." He said in a husky voice. He was tall, light-skinned with green eyes and long brown dreadlocks pushed back in a neat ponytail. God, he was handsome as ever.

As he walked in, Graceful came out of his bedroom. He stopped in his tracks and peeped in the living room to see what we were doing. He noticed Cameo and Queeney and the strange nameless man. The man in return stared back at Graceful. They didn't exchange words. It was all in a look—a stern, hard stare that was piercing. A wide-eyed look with brows rose like winning the lottery. They were locked in this look for what seemed like minutes like it was a contest of some sort.

As soon as Graceful turned around to head back inside of his bedroom, there were three loud knocks at the door. The knocks were so loud and hard everybody stopped what they were doing, our eyes were glued toward the door. And with a flash of a second, the clean-shaven man pulled out a gun and pointed it at Graceful.

"FREEZE! FBI...NOBODY MOVE!" The light-skinned agent shrieked. Then there was a loud BOOM that followed at the door, and a stampede of feet ambushed in like cockroaches. Several agents dressed in black with FBI in bold yellow letters on the front of their shirts grabbed each person and manhandled us face down to the floor. All we could see were the color of their eyes through the ski masks. Graceful ran toward his bedroom and yelled to Jada Million, "5-O!" Graceful managed to get to his bedroom. He tried to shut the door but the light-skinned agent was right on his heels and stuck his lean muscle-bound body in the door before it could close. He used all of his might to bust the door wide open and slammed Graceful to the floor and cuffed him. Then the agent pointed his index finger towards Jada Million. "*You*...get down on the floor! If you move, I'll shoot," he told him in a militant tone. As the light-skinned agent was handling his business, the other agents searched every crevasse of the house. They found cocaine, at least twenty firearms, weed, ecstasy, heroin, and bundles of money wrapped in Christmas wrapping paper. The agents confiscated about $300,000.00 in cash as well as the Cadillacs. The other agents loaded all of us ladies in the patty wagon. The light-skinned agent told Graceful, "You're finished. We got your pimping ass now. Your pimping days are over!" Graceful remained quiet, and when he did speak all he said was, "I want to call my lawyer."

"Oh, you'll get your chance to call your lawyer, don't worry." The light-skinned agent said in a smug tone. "Check all those whores for warrants," he told the other agents, "we gonna need statements from all of 'em. If they refuse, tell 'em they going down with the pimp. That will get 'em to talk like fuckin' canaries."

Down at the Paterson Precinct, Graceful was booked on possession, possessions with the intent to distribute a controlled substance, pandering, promoting prostitution, white slavery, transporting minors across state lines for the purpose of prostitution, endangering the welfare of a minor, and statutory rape. His bail was set at one million dollars. His bail had major stipulations on cash and his bail bonds.

Some of the girls had warrants. Other girls were making statements that Graceful was their pimp to save their own asses. Some were runaways lured into the world of prostitution. Others were homeless looking for shelter and were persuaded with the perks of food and a hot shower, a TV to watch, and a warm bed to sleep in. Every girl had her own reasons for getting sucked in and when we realized what we had gotten ourselves into, we wanted out but it was too late. A debt had to be paid for all the luxuries and benefits Graceful had treated us to. We had to use our God given looks, body, and talents to pay off our debts. Sex was the only way to make some fast cash and please Daddy. We knew that as long as Daddy was happy, all was well, and we'd live to see another day.

Stripping, exotic dancing, prostitution was none of our aspirations. We were all underage when we got into the industry. Most of us were from fatherless homes, drug-addicted parents, or someone in the family had molested us. One girl mother had pimped her out and she knew nothing more than selling her body. Another girl had deceased parents like me and she had no other family to turn to, like me, so as you know we turned to the streets hoping to find someone to love us, someone to care for us, someone to comfort us. At least I did have Fat Boy and his mom up until things got…well, you know the story.

Graceful was on the lookout for the weak and vulnerable, damaged and distressed, burdened and dismantled girls and he embraced each of us with open arms with a different objective in mind. A lot of us couldn't see, we were yearning for a father's love, and Graceful was the closest to a daddy any of us would come close to having.

I think all of us could've done without the abuse, though. The abuse only broke us down to be feeble young girls, which would only create feeble young women if we didn't find the tools to build ourselves up after being torn down so low on the strip pole.

Down at the precinct all of us ladies were assured that Graceful was the main target. Of course we were accessories to the crime. According to the Feds, Graceful had been under surveillance for about a year. It was a joyous occasion for them after bringing Graceful down. They were clapping, laughing, and giving each other high-fives and whatnot. It was crazy.

I laid on the cot in the rear of the cell. I was praying that the Feds didn't find out that I had a fake ID. As I lay there and looked at my surroundings, it was then that I realized no more. No more dancing, stripping, hoeing… absolutely, no more. I was tired. My body was tired. My mind was tired. My soul was tired. Yeah. I was depleted of this thing called Hoe Living. My days with Graceful and this life that had literally drained me…I was done.

The Feds asked me to sign a statement against Graceful, but I refused. I knew that they would have to release me. I didn't have a warrant, and I knew that all they wanted was Graceful, and all I wanted more than anything in the world was to regain my life back. Don't get me wrong; I was a little apprehensive about my decision about not writing that statement. I mean things could've easily gone left on me instead of right, but I had this gut instinct and I followed that. Even though I never loved Graceful, I felt sorry for him. He had a lot of connections in the tri-state area. And even though he beat me senselessly, I couldn't find it in my heart to hate him. Call me stupid, I don't care, but I had to do what was best for Alice, not Desire.

I promised myself that if I ever got out of this mess

that I was in I would get my GED and go to college. I wanted to rekindle my relationship with Fat Boy. I had a little money stashed away that would hold me over until I found a job and a place of my own.

"Alice Banks," this white officer called out. "You're being released on your own recognizance. All you have to do is report back on your court date. Sign here and they'll begin your process to be released." He told me.

The first thing I did when I got out of jail was to buy a newspaper. Graceful's face was plastered all over the front page of the Herald News:

TRI-STATE KING PIMP BUSTED!

They raised Graceful's bail to five million dollars. They sure don't want him to get out, I said to myself. Then I thought about Egypt. She had been detained for warrants: shoplifting, prostitution, and she was listed as a runaway. Reality really sunk in about how blessed I was, not lucky, but blessed. Why was I the chosen one, I wondered? How come they didn't hold me, I asked myself. I mean I'd done the devil's work too. I'd done things that I was ashamed of admitting, no different from Egypt. What was God trying to tell me, huh? Was He saying, "Alice, my child, you have been through an obstacle of life lessons but I am willing to give you another chance because you are worthy of one." I felt myself getting choked up just by the thought of God saying that to me—me, the girl who had lost so much, including herself. And He was willing to overlook all of my indiscretions and give me, me, another chance. No one could tell me that God wasn't good. No one.

I sat in Grill 77 on Washington Street and ate a cheese steak sandwich with a side order of French fries and a Cola, pondering over everything I had endured. After eating I decided to call the one person I thought could help me...Fat Boy's mom. I needed to reach out to someone and as you know I didn't have many options. I had to swallow all pride and take a leap of faith, so I did.

I called Candy and asked if she could meet me at the Paterson Free Public Library on Broadway. I told her that I needed to talk to her, to confide in her. She agreed to meet me. I can't tell you how afraid I was. I was afraid to admit my wrongs to her. I loved her son very much and the last thing I wanted to do was hurt him. I didn't want to hurt him but somehow I did. I regretted him ever finding out but then I thought about it and I realized that things happen for a reason. Maybe it was best that the truth was leaked out. Just maybe, this might all work in my favor, I thought. I had to remain humble about everything I was about to do. I had to remember the pain and suffering to keep me grounded. I had to remember how it felt to be dismissed by the boy I loved with mind, body, and soul. I had to taste it on the tip of my tongue. I had to taste it, no matter how bitter it was. I had to in order to redeem myself and grow into the young woman I knew I could be. My mama didn't raise no fool and it was time for me to acknowledge that.

Around 1:20 p.m., Candy walked in with Jada on her arm. She was dressed casual, something different because most of the time when I saw her she was always in her nurse uniform. She looked nice, relaxed in the face like she coming into her own again. Jada was all smiles when she spotted me sitting in the rear of the library reading a book. I stood and greeted the both of them.

"Hi."

"Alice," Jada sang my name so full of joy.

It felt good to be acknowledged.

"How old are you now?" I asked Jada.

"Ten." She said in her little voice.

I remember when I was ten, oh, do I remember, I thought to myself.

Candy and I sat down while Jada ran downstairs to the children's department to get on the computer.

"Well," I started off to say, "Um," I took several deeps

breaths feeling like I was about to faint, not from my fainting spells but from anxiety. This was tough, seeing Candy again; her piercing eyes staring into mine. "I asked you to come so that I could talk, explain, I mean talk about…"

"Take your time, Alice," Candy said so compassionately.

I was a complete basket case, trying to figure out what words to use to explain how I was feeling, what I had been through, how I felt about Fat Boy, I was tongue-tied.

I took another deep, deep, deep breath.

"I'm sorry." I said, "I'm so sorry for any pain I might've caused you and your family. I love your son with everything in me. You gotta believe that." Tears engulfed in my eyes because I was sincerely pouring my heart and soul out to her. "Things, there's so much that has happened. I messed up. I messed up big." I lowered my head feeling this abundance of weight on my shoulders. God, the weight was heavy.

Candy reached her hand out to me. I reached in for hers. "Listen, I know that you love my son. I can see it in your eyes; I hear it in your voice. How are you doing, Alice? How are you really doing?" she asked me.

"Honestly, I don't know. There's so much…I'm alone. I mean I feel so lonely. There's no one left for me to…"

"For you to… what?" Candy asked with a concerned look in her eyes.

"For me to go to. There's so much…" I repeated again.

"Talk to me, Alice. Tell me what's troubling you," she said.

So I did. I told her the whole story, any and everything that Fat Boy might've left out, I told her.

"Listen, my home is always open to you," Candy said, "we'd like for you to come stay with us. Would you like that?"

I was a bucket of tears. I couldn't compose myself. It was like words that I had been dying to hear for so long.

Having a place to call "home" was like I'd died and gone to friggin' heaven. Yeah. Heaven.

***

New York, New York

Harry Humphrey, a managing partner for twenty-fives years sat at his desk bombarded with paperwork. He removed his bifocals and leaned back in his chair with a perplexed look upon his fifty-seven year old face.

"'Ey, Tom." Harry said scratching his bushy blonde beard.

"Yeah." Tom LaRousse, a forty-two year old insurance agent responded while shaking the toner at the copier.

"Have you had any luck with the Banks file yet?"

"No, sir. Michele Banks had one child named Alice that she put as her beneficiary. According to my records, Alice should be 18 now. But I'm having a problem trying to locate her. Michele only received one payment of $20,000.00 about four or fives years ago. The remaining balance on the policy is $180,000.00 owed to her next of kin, which is her daughter."

"Okay, I file a motion with the courts and let the judge decide what we should do until Alice is found or comes forth." Harry said.

"Yes, sir." Tom said, while hitting the "start" button on the copier.

"What a shame...Michele was killed in that horrendous fashion years ago." Harry said, while pinching the inner corners of his eyes. "Her parents were very nice people."

Tom nodded his head, still standing at the copier retrieving his pile of papers for the policy he was working on. "Who notified you of her death?" Tom asked. "Her ex-boyfriend Randy. I got a call from him a year after her premature passing. Says he lives in Georgia somewhere."

Harry explained. "Randy said Michele informed him of the life insurance policy (when they were on good terms) should anything happen to her. She gave him all the information."

"Talk about premonition." Tom said. *Wow, there's someone out there who has $180,000.00 just sitting here and she doesn't even know it*, Tom thought to himself.

After retrieving his papers, Tom walked back to his cluttered desk, and sat his lean body down and began making calls.

The Banks would rollover in their graves if they knew the chain of events that led up to Michele's death," Harry thought to himself, while staring out of the dusty window.

Tom hung up the phone, "No luck there," he said. He knew that it would be like trying to find a needle in a haystack recovering Alice Banks.

***

Mid State Correctional Facility

Candy, Jada, and I were leaving the prison. All in all it was a good visit. We brought Fat Boy a home cooked meal. I know he missed his mom's cooking. It had been six month's and Fat Boy had put our relationship on pause. Although it bothered me I hung in there to show him that I meant well. 'Ey I made a huge mistake but I owned up to it. I didn't run and hide like a little baby. Honestly, I was tired of running from my problems. I loved him and I knew that he loved me. True love didn't dissipate that quickly. At least, I didn't want to believe that it did. I wanted Fat Boy in the worst way but I had to be patient about it. He was hurt and so was I on so many levels for so many different reasons. I'd hoped that he could see that but I knew that it was going to take some time, some healing, and I had to regain his trust.

With everything in us, Fat Boy and I decided to salvage our relationship. It was rocky, at first. But the love we still felt for one another kind of helped us both realize what was important. Everyone didn't have what we had. To us, it was worth another chance.

I was on a regimen of me, getting back into school which meant gaining a diploma or GED. I enrolled in this program called NJ Youth Initiative Corp., downtown Paterson. I managed to get a job under the table at a thrift store. I had to start off small and work my way up.

It took about six months to a year in the NJ Youth Initiative Corp. program to gain my diploma. It was well worth the extra time. With the little experience I attained from the thrift store I managed to get hired for a part-time position as a Customer Service Representative for an Adolescent Hotline Service. Go figure? I felt like I was making a difference by helping young girls and boys. It really hit me when this one boy called in stating that his girlfriend was whooping his ass. He was crying and everything over the phone. I tried with everything in me not to laugh, but it was rather funny. Not funny, ha-ha, but funny, that "boys" got their asses kicked too. Wow. It was unheard of to me. Goes to show how sheltered I was.

I told Fat Boy about my job, he'd never heard of Customer Service Representative before. I basically told him that I answered phones all day and listened to people's problems and tried to comfort them. Most of the calls I got were from young girls around my age or younger. I kid you not, I surely could relate to some of their stories—horrific, tragic, and painful stories. It so brought back memories. I truly believed that God intended this for me, as a way of giving back to the universe or something.

Anyway, Fat Boy's appeal was coming along just fine. Mr. Myles had informed him that he still had a good chance at winning his case. Reason being was because he was trying to protect his mother. It had been five years that Fat Boy had been incarcerated—five long agonizing years.

Candy had to often preach to Fat Boy about him getting into so much trouble, mostly the fighting. He was like a firecracker behind prison bars. The anger would just erupt and no one could get through to him—no one. Mr. Myles also told Fat Boy that he needed to walk a straight-line and keep his nose clean as possible. All of this would play a big part when it came time for him to go before the Appeal board. I knew to him it felt like Judgment Day. Every day felt like that to me.

Well, Fat Boy agreed to try his hardest. But knowing how angry he could get, it wasn't going to be easy. I wouldn't say that it was impossible, because I believed that he could do any and all things he put his mind to. Yeah. I was his biggest supporter.

***

I received an unexpected call from a woman named Mary, which happened to be Graceful's sister. I had never met or seen Mary the whole time I was living in the house. She informed me that I could come to the house and gather my belongings if I wanted to. I jumped at the chance but my money was starting to look funny. I told her that I would come the following day, which was a Thursday at noon. She agreed to meet me.

Going back to the house felt strange to me. I never thought I would ever step foot back in that house, but I did. I rung the doorbell and this obese woman with shoulder length hair and the darkest skin I'd ever seen answered the door dressed in a bathrobe and leopard slippers. As soon as she saw my face, she smiled.

"Hi. I'm Alice, you called me about picking up my belongings." I said.

"Oh, yes, please come on in." She said in the most pleasant southern tone I'd ever heard. She most definitely was the opposite of her brother.

"My name is Mary."

"Nice to meet you." I said to her as I headed toward my old bedroom. Mary had followed me. But I paid her no mind. It seemed Graceful had informed her about us girls and things that needed to be tended to at the house.

As I entered the bedroom, I felt this disconnection like I had parted ways with that house. All the bad memories had seemingly disappeared. It was the weirdest feeling I had ever encountered.

"Um, you know, Alice, my brother needs your help." Mary said subtly.

I walked over to the bed and lifted the mattress to retrieve the picture I had left behind. It was still wrapped in the plastic and in pretty good condition. As I gaped at the picture I found myself daydreaming about a time so long ago. My eyes began to get misty. I opened the dresser drawers to get some of my undergarments, jeans, socks, two pairs of high-heeled shoes, a designer bag, and some toiletries. Mary tried to break my train of thought, while I was stuffing my satchel. "You okay, chile? You listening to me, I said my brother needs your help," she said in a melancholy tone. I practically ignored her. Then walked right passed her as if her 350 pounds were invisible with my belongings and picture clenched in my hands.

As I exited the house, I thought, help! He needs *my* help? He's going to need more than my help to get him out of this jam he's in. And it was the absolute truth.

A couple of month's later, I had heard that they were trying to give Graceful like 100 years or something like that. He knew and I knew that his days of pimping were over and my days of dancing were over too.

Come January, I was starting community college in Paramus, New Jersey, majoring in Accounting. I couldn't wait! I wanted to live on campus but I didn't know if I'd be able to afford it. I had taken out for a grant, which was basically free money to help pay for my tuition. I applied for any and every type of financial aid, they had. The last thing I wanted to do was to apply for a student loan but if I had to I had to. I figured six months after I graduated then I'd be obligated to pay the money back, hopefully I'd land a good paying job. Getting into the swing of things in college was pretty tough for me. My study habits were atrocious. My attention span was terrible. Reading skills were minimal. My math was just as bad. I had no idea how difficult college could be to a novice, but after about four months I had gotten a routine down. It took time to adjust to my new surroundings, but eventually I did. My grades along with my confidence picked up.

As a sophomore, I decided to move on campus. My dorm roommate was this girl from Ridgefield Park named Jessica Rodriguez. She was Puerto Rican but she was mad cool. She was majoring in Psychology. Fat Boy didn't like the idea of me living on campus, but I explained to him that the commute was killing me financially. I was living on a budget. It took a lot of convincing but finally Fat Boy supported my decision. It wasn't like he couldn't come and visit me once he got out of prison. Truthfully, I think me meeting new people might've made him feel a little left out. But I loved him more than anyone I'd known. He just had to believe it, not by my words, but more so by my actions.

After a few months I landed a job at the college in the Bursar office. Eventually I was tired of walking everywhere I went, so I decided to study to get my driver's license. It took at least three tries before I passed the friggin' driver's test to get my permit. I called one of those driver's school to practice driving on the weekends. Around July, I took the road test and passed with flying colors. Probably about another month or two, I bought a used champagne-colored Honda Civic that was in mint condition. The owner who sold it to me was this little old white lady from Teaneck, New Jersey. It had minimal miles on it. The interior was practically new, but the car had the stench of mothballs. Other than that everything was good. I mean considering everything I had already been through I was doing better than I expected.

I found myself sharing some of my life battles, hardships, and loss with some of the students I befriended. Most of 'em couldn't believe the shit I had gone through. One girl named Madeline, who was tall as a friggin' tree with sea blue eyes and wavy blonde hair looked like the girls I've seen on TV soaking up the sun on Malibu Beach. Ironically, Madeline was a native of California. She said that her parents divorced when she was nine years old and she and her mom moved to New Jersey. I cannot remember what she majored in though.

Anyway, Madeline suggested that I write a book about my life. "I don't think it would be entertaining enough. I think people would get bored and use my book as a bedpost." I told her. I didn't laugh, smirk, or smile when I told her that. Nope. I was dead serious. Who would want to read about constant misery, anguish, neglect, betrayal, huh? If I didn't live the life I sure as hell wouldn't want to hear about it, let alone read about it from prologue to chapter one through forty-one, that's for sure.

Madeline swooped her long blonde hair to the side with her index finger. "Alice, you'd be surprised how many of us girls have experienced what you have here on this campus," she said. "You should do it! I'd be your first buyer," she assured me. "Do you know how many women have gone through tragedy and used their pain as a voice," she concluded, trying to persuade me to see things her way. I didn't, at first, but her words, her positive energy had me going for a brief moment.

I chuckled but deep down I wondered if Madeline was trying to tell me something about herself on the sneak tip. She had me thinking about it. How quickly did the thoughts sweep through my mind like an abrupt wind and then dissipate like yesterday. Suddenly it was gone. Me being a writer, let alone a best selling author. C'mon.

Honestly, till this day I don't know why I was sharing my stories. But I do know that it wasn't for fame, that's for sure. It could've been as a way for me to heal, to find closure within myself. Who knows?

I told myself not to concern myself with the past. The past was just that, the past. I had to look forward toward my future, which was school and Fat Boy's appeal. Those were my *only* two concerns.

The appeal was a slow and grueling process for all of us, especially Fat Boy. Mr. Myles had assured us that we would hear something within 24 months. Two years seemed like eternity to me. Fat Boy and I constantly wrote letters to one another. So did his mom and his sister Jada. Candy wrote letters to the appeal board, parole board, judge, the governor, and to anyone who would lend an open ear. Everyone fought hard for Fat Boy's release.

It was 7 years now that Fat Boy had been incarcerated. Mr. Myles said that it was a 60/40 chance that the conviction would be overturned in Fat Boy's favor. Fat Boy told me and Candy that as long as we didn't give up on him, and continued to write and visit that he could do the time.

***

I was on my way to Candy's house, this particular day. I think it might've been a Friday. Most of the time I would spend my weekends or free time over there, if I didn't have to work. Jada and I had become very close. She looked up to me, asked for my advice and opinions on things. She even told me that she wanted to be just like me especially since I started going to college. I remember telling her to never want to be like someone else but to always try to improve the person that you are. Happiness comes from within. Can't nobody define your happiness but you. I was trying to be a role model to her in spite of my past. It felt good to be considered a "big sister". Real good.

After leaving Candy's house and heading back to the college, I cut down this side street to avoid construction that was going on, on Broadway. I stopped at the red light jamming to some Mary J. Blige when I noticed this girl who looked so familiar to me. The girl looked a hot mess, but I swear I knew her. Her body was emaciated. Her wife beater T and hot pink spandex was holey and dingy. Her hair was knotty. Her skin was sunken in with dark spots and sores on it. As she was walking passed the front of my car, she started doing what looked like the "crack dance" in the middle of the street. I kept beeping my horn for her to get her dirty ass out of the middle of the street. Beep! Beep! Beep! This chick wouldn't budge, she just kept on dancing without a care in the fuckin' world.

Finally she got her dingy ass out of the way, but as she walked I took a better look at her and noticed that she was none other than Egypt. We both made eye contact. I hit the breaks nearly having the car behind me crash into me but the driver swerved around me. I took a deep breath, then pulled over and rolled down my window and stuck my head out to call out to her. "EGYPT! EGYPT! EGYPT, it's Alice." Egypt dropped her head as she walked over to my car. She patted her knotty hair down like she was primping in a mirror and wiped her hands across her dry, chapped lips. I got out of my car and we embraced in a hug. I started crying. So did she. It was a touching moment for us both.

"Where you headed?" I asked her. "You need a ride anywhere?"

Egypt remained silent like she was embarrassed or something.

"You wanna come ride with me. I'm on my way to the park." I was really on my way back to school.

Egypt nodded her head yes and we both jumped in my car and headed to Van Saun Park in Paramus to get away from the hustle and bustle. I stopped at Wendy's on our way to the park to get a bite to eat.

I parked the car by this gigantic tree at Van Saun Park and Egypt and I talked for what seemed like five hours. We reminisced about our past lives, way before Graceful came into the picture. We laughed. We cried some more. We talked about when we were little girls. How I used to come over to her house and eat there when there was no food at my house. How Egypt's grandmother would cook good food and bring food over to my house. We talked about old man Fred at the DP station. We talked about any and everything under the sun. Egypt talked about all the years she'd spent with Graceful and how her life came to her becoming a crackhead. It was the most profound conversation I think we'd ever had.

Egypt and I had a history together. And even though she was a crackhead and I was a college student didn't make me any better than her. I didn't look down on her. I wanted her to know that I was still her girl.

"Prison was hard, Alice." Egypt said.

"How much time did you have to serve," I asked her.

"A little less than a year. After that I started hanging with the wrong crowd of people, then started smoking crack. I thought I could handle it, you know. I started Go-Go dancing at the Chyna Club and using cocaine. But after a while, all I found myself wanting to do was smoke crack."

I didn't know exactly what to say so all I did was listen, unless she asked for my opinion on something. It was difficult to hear her story. After our mouths grew dry, I gave Egypt my cell phone number.

"Call me whenever you want to, okay." I told her.

She nodded her head up and down with tears streaming heavy down her face. I reached over and gave her a tight squeeze and assured her that she would get herself back on track but she had to want to want better.

"I want better, Alice, I really do. It's tough, especially

when everyone around you is getting high."

"Not trying to be funny, E, but you have to change your surroundings, the people you hang with, and the things you do for recreation. It's all up to you and only you. I can't make you stop no one can, but you."

"I promise, I'm gonna stop, Alice." She said in a soft-spoken tone.

I can't say if I believed her or not. Time would definitely tell.

We both hugged again with tears now streaming down both of our faces. Our emotions really got the better of us that day, but I think that's how it was meant to be. I was supposed to bump into Egypt and extend some words of wisdom. I let her know that she was not alone.

"'Ey, Alice, you still be having those fainting spells."

"I only fainted once in the last two years."

Egypt started coughing uncontrollably.

"Are you all right, E? That cough doesn't sound good at all. When was the last time you've been to see a doctor?"

"I dunno. I was checked once while in prison."

"Well, you need to see a doctor soon."

Egypt nodded her head.

Around 6:30 p.m., we headed back to Paterson for me to drop Egypt off.

"Where do you live?" I asked her.

Egypt didn't respond.

"Where would you like for me to drop you off at?" I said.

"Oh. You can drop me off on the next block," she said.

I pulled over and dropped her off across from the Presbyterian Church. We hugged again, and then Egypt got out of the car and strutted her bony ass down the street but before I pulled off I heard Egypt calling out for me. I stopped the car, as she walked up to it. I rolled down the passenger side window. "What's up?" Egypt was looking at the seat but there was nothing there. "I have to tell you something, Alice, but I don't know how to say it to you."

She said. "Don't worry, girl, call me tonight and tell me then." "Okay. I'll call you later, Alice. I love you." Egypt said.

"I love you, too."

Egypt walked off and I headed back to Paramus.

As Egypt walked away she knew what she had to divulge to Alice would hurt her as well as damage what was left of their friendship. How am I going to tell her that it was me who wrote the letter to Fat Boy? She thought to herself. It was a heavy burden that she was carrying around on her shoulders and buried in her chest. She regretted doing it, but she wanted to come clean hoping that it wouldn't jeopardize what they shared. It wasn't like Egypt had a lot of friends. Everyone that she knew pretty much shunned her.

***

I was in my junior year and things were going rather well for me. I hadn't heard from Egypt like she promised. She never called. I was really disappointed in her for not keeping her word. I wondered what had happened to her. It was like she dropped off the face of the earth. It was six months later, when this girl named Tiffany Highman, a sophomore who knew *her*, not personally, but knew of her from the neighborhood, stopped me in the hall as I was heading to my next class, and pulled me to the side to tell me some disturbing news.

"It's a shame, right?" Tiffany said with sadness in her face.

"What?" I asked her.

"About that young girl who died." she said.

"What girl?"

"That girl that lived in Paterson. I saw her with my cousin Mecca one time."

"Who Shay?"

"No. The other girl, um, Egypt."

I tell you I liked to die right then and there. My mouth hung wide open and tears just flowed from my eyes. I was in shock. My heart was beating so fast. I was a nervous wreck. I ended up cutting class and drove to Paterson to see if I could find her mom. I was hoping that they still lived at the same residence. I wanted to find out if this news was true and if it was I wanted to express my condolences.

Once I arrived back to my neck of the woods, seeing the house that I grew up in had me frazzled. Old memories crept back in my head. I was literally paralyzed sitting in the driver's seat. My palms gripped the steering wheel as I started hyperventilating. I rolled down the window to get some air because I was so nauseous. If Egypt weren't my friend I would have never returned back to that block. My whole body was quivering as I opened the car door. I could barely step out of my car I was so distraught. I took one deep breath and then I just stepped out, took another breath, and then headed towards Egypt's house.

I rung the door, but no one answered right away. As I was about to leave I saw someone peep out of the first floor window. It looked like Egypt's mom, but I wasn't for certain. By the time I started heading down the stairs and stepped on the third step, I heard the front door squeak open.

"Can I help you?" This feeble female voice said.

I turned around and there who stood before me was this thin woman with dark spots all over her face. It was most definitely her mom. And she looked like she was still drugging too. "Yes, I am looking for Egypt." I told her.

The woman broke down in tears in the doorway. That's when I knew that it was true. Egypt was dead.

"Ma'am, are you okay?" I asked her.

"My baby's dead," she said weeping like she was dying inside. "Her wake is on Thursday. The viewing will be from 3-5 and 5-7 at Bragg Funeral Home. The funeral will be on Friday. How do you know my daughter?" she asked me in a crackling voice.

"She was my best friend. My name is Alice...Alice Banks."

"Are you the child that used to live in that house right there?" She pointed her long, thin finger to the house next door.

"Yes, ma'am."

"Oh, dear God." She said as she raised her thin hands up to her mouth like she had seen a ghost.

"Well, ma'am, I don't want to take up too much of your time.

"No, baby, you're not taking up my time. I'm glad you stopped by. I hope to see you at the wake."

"Yes, ma'am. I'll be there."

As I walked toward my car, I felt her still standing in the doorway watching me walk away and get into my car and drive off.

I took off that semester from school. There was no way I could function knowing that my best friend had died. Of course I was curious as to what her cause of death was but I didn't feel it was appropriate to ask her mom. I stayed at Candy's house instead of at the dorm. I needed to be around family. Candy offered to go with me to the wake and funeral. Boy was I relieved because I knew that I didn't want to go alone. If Fat Boy were home he would've gone with me. But he wasn't.

Word on the streets said that Egypt had died from pneumonia. Other rumors said that she was HIV-positive and had died from AIDS related complications. Honestly, I didn't know what was true or false. All I did know was that the rumors were pretty consistent.

Bragg Funeral Home was damn near empty the day of the wake. Only a few family members and friends showed up to pay their respects. I was pissed off about that. It was a sad occasion and half of the people Egypt knew couldn't find it within their hearts to come and show compassion for the deceased. Candy, Jada, and I sat in the front row. We sent three bouquets of red carnations beforehand because I wasn't sure if her mom could afford to. I stood and said some kind words about my friend as I stared at her picture that was embroidered in what looked like a rug that could be hung up on your wall or used as a throw. Egypt had a big Kool-Aid smile on her face.

Egypt's mom was hysterical. I guessed so many thoughts raced through her head about how much time was wasted between them. Egypt had to grow up beyond her years, and her mom missed out on those years because of her drug addiction. She took it hard. She was falling on the floor bawling her eyes out. Trying to pull her daughter's body out of the casket. She even tried to get in the casket with her, while screaming with bulging eyes and big tears and clear snot running down her nose, hysterically screaming at the top of her lungs, "My baby's gone! She's gone!" God, it was so hard to watch her literally have a nervous breakdown right before our eyes. I felt so sorry for her.

Egypt was twenty-one when she died. It really woke me up as to how a life could be taken so easily. It made me think about my mom. From what I knew, Michele never had a proper wake or funeral. There was no one to identify her. Most of the time when that happens the deceased is labeled a Jane Doe. I promised myself that one day, after all of this mayhem in my life blows over that I'd try to locate my mom's whereabouts and give her a proper burial.

***

Fat Boy sat in his cell playing chess with his cellmate

Saabs. "Checkmate!" Saabs said. "Man, am I playing alone or what. You seem distracted. What's up?"

"Nothing." Fat Boy said staring into space.

"It must be something because I beat you this time." Saabs told him. "Look man, whatever is on your mind let it go. If things are able to distract you like this then you need to cut those ties loose. Disconnect yourself from it and move the fuck on."

"Yeah, man whatever." Fat Boy said just to get Saabs off of his back. All Fat Boy had been thinking about was Graceful. He found out that Graceful had been transferred to Mid State Correctional Facility. The last thing Fat Boy wanted to do was to be looking the pimp who turned his girl out in the face. He knew eventually Graceful and him would one day cross paths.

It didn't take long for Fat Boy to confide in Saabs about the letter that was anonymously written. He shared personal information about how Alice was trickin' for this pimp named Graceful. "Man, I'm gonna fuck him up when I see him!" Fat Boy was pacing back and forth across the floor with his flip-flocks slapping against his sweat socks. Saabs tried to reason with him, "Listen Fat, you better leave that nigga alone. They say that pimp got like 50 years. He doesn't have anything to lose." Fat Boy remained quiet. Saabs continued hoping that he was getting through to him. "And plus, your appeal is coming up soon. Think about your mom, your girl, and your sister. Your girl loves you. Man, don't throw all of that away over nothing."

Fat Boy face scowled. "Whatchu mean…nothing! That pimp turned my girl out! He had her stripping and selling her pussy. You call that nothing!" Fat Boy snapped.

Saabs was always rationalizing things. "Answer this, Fat, did he force her? Did he put a gun to her head and make her strip? Listen, I'm just giving you my opinion, man. Being a whore is by choice, not force. Your girl could've stepped to him. She might've been down and out with no money and nowhere to go. You know how that shit goes. A pimp meets a girl, either she's out there fucking niggas for free. Her stepfather might've been whipping her ass or even worse he might've raped her. Or she might've just wanted to be grown, tired of following rules at home and just bounced. Or she might've just liked and wanted the pimp and hoe lifestyle. You never know what leads a female to become a whore. It is a million reasons why women turn to pimps, but one thing I know, none of those reasons are the pimps' fault. Now he might've come along way with some slick and smooth talk and nice clothes. He might've even had a nice car and showoff his diamonds and shit, but like I said, Fat, it's not his fault."

"I don't give a fuck!" Fat Boy snapped back. "He fucked with the wrong nigga's girl. And he got to pay. And best believe he will pay as soon as I get the chance. He put my girl out there and he's the reason she has fainting spells and shit. Yeah, he whipped her ass so much that she has fainting spells. Now what kind of man would I be if I had the chance and I didn't get some payback for my lady, huh?"

"Okay, Fat, do what you feel. I'm done talkin' about it." Saabs said frazzled. "You're young…"

Fat Boy sucked his teeth. "That maybe so…I thought you said you was done talkin' about it."

Saabs just looked at him cross-eyed. "You wrong man."

"Shut up, nigga. And make your move." Fat Boy contested with this smug look on his face.

"Man, I already made my move earlier. Didn't you hear me say checkmate?"

Fat Boy had a dumfound look on his face. "Oh. My bad."

***

176

While I was getting dressed in my dorm room, my girlfriends Beverly, Tasha, Nikki and Casey were teasing me. It was really Nikki who instigated everything. "Girl, I don't know why you looking so damn depressed these days. Your man is in jail. Look, you gotta life too. Loving him is okay, but I mean c'mon, you need some dick, bitch." Nikki with her anorexic ass looking like Olive Ole twin sister looked at me with her big ass blue eyes and thin lips all twisted up like she was amazed that I was still functioning. Nikki was a bonafide hoe. She was the talk of the campus for like a month when I first enrolled. "Seriously, how long has it been now?" Casey asked with a perplexed look upon her pimpled, brown-skinned face. Before I could answer, Beverly took the liberty of speaking for me. "Too long." Everyone broke out in laughter. Beverly was tall, but she was wide-hipped and she was pretty too. She had long blond hair with cocoa-brown eyes and deep dimples. She was down-to-earth too, but nosey as hell with other peoples business but let it be her, oh, she'd have a freakin' attitude if we clowned her. Some people can't see their flaws and Beverly was definitely one of those people.

I didn't see anything wrong with practicing abstinence. I mean it wasn't like Fat Boy was having his cake and eating it too. We were both in the same predicament as far as I was concerned. Neither one of us was getting any. I felt bad not being able to feed my body, and yes, my body was in urgent need of the feel and touch of a man, but I loved Fat Boy to death. And I didn't want to do anything that would hurt him. I mean the thought had crossed my mind about busting a coupla nuts and having one good orgasm. I was most definitely tired of pleasuring myself. It wasn't as fulfilling as having a dick between my legs. Pleasuring myself would just take the edge off, but by mid-week I'd be horny all over again. My body was starving but I was not trying to get caught up in anything that might jeopardize my relationship with Fat Boy. I almost lost him once.

Anyway, that particular day I had a date with this guy named Keith Alexander. He was attending the same college. I forgot what he was majoring in. It had something to do with medicine, I do recall, but I don't remember if he said that he wanted to be a doctor or not. Keith was nice. He stood about 6'1" with sexy brown eyes and flawless light skin with curly velvety brunette hair. He was muscular with gorgeous features. He could've been a model that's how good-looking he was. He asked me out to the movies. It was purely innocent, but not innocent enough to let Fat Boy know. I hadn't been on a real date since Fat Boy had taken me to New York City. That seemed so long ago. So the girls were ragging on me because I finally had a prospect and they didn't want me to screw it up. Beverly distracted my train of thought. "Girl, you better go and get that dick because I am tired of your ass walking around here grouchy and irritable all the time. And make sure that nigga can lick it first, bitch." I rolled my eyes over at her. Then quiet little Tasha joined in. "You know he eat pussy with those luscious lips of his. Stop actin' like you don't know." I was shocked to hear her say something like that to me. Tasha was the little black church girl of the crew. She was dark-skinned with a body like Janet Jackson. Yeah. The girl was fine, but she didn't act conceited. She just had a dirty mouth. There was always one girl in a bunch that had mad mouth but when it came down to showing and proving herself she'd clam up. Well, that was Tasha for sure. Some of the boys on campus considered her to be a tease. They'd say she was all talk and no action. Sometimes I wondered if she knew how pretty she really was. I guess if I were as fine as she was I probably wouldn't smell my own shit. "Shut up with ya'll nasty asses." I yelled across the room at all of them. "You guys are some nasty heifers." "But we ain't the one horny, you are." Beverly said with a sly grin on her face. "Alice, keep it real. You know your man got a girl on the side." Beverly cut her eyes at the other girls. She nodded her head too. "He got a girl up in there. You know what they say…" Before I had a chance to respond to Beverly's sly comment there was a knock at the door. Beverly, Tasha, Nikki, and Casey jumped up and started pushing me toward the door. They were giggling like schoolgirls and whatnot and pulling on me at the same time. I screamed, "Get offa me you nasty tricks!" They were really laughing then. Before I closed the door one of them, it sounded like Beverly yelled, "Lick and stick, lick and stick…" I tried to hurry up and shut the door before Keith heard her trifling ass.

***

It was my senior year. I could not believe that I was scheduled to graduate on time, but I was. I can't tell you how proud I was of myself. Through everything I had been through I managed to stay focused and apply everything I had in my studies and it paid off. For once in my life I felt like I had accomplished something good. But suddenly that good feeling started to fade before my eyes as I felt myself slipping out of consciousness. Everything was black before my eyes as if someone had turned off a nightlight.

When I finally came to I found myself in the emergency room of Hackensack University Medical Center. Apparently I had another fainting spell. It had been about three years since I had a spell. Doctors ran tests on me. They contacted the doctors from St. Joseph's Regional Medical Center to find out about my medical history. They informed the doctor of the aneurysm. I had long stopped taking my medication and going for my annual checkups like I was supposed to do. I called myself trying to self-medicate myself by not following the rules of my doctor. And that got me nowhere but back to the drawing board.

This white nurse with bright highlights in her dirty blonde hair had asked me for a next of kin to call in case of an emergency. I told her to call Candy since she was the only family I had. Dr. Steele, a pale-skinned dark-haired neurologist with the sexiest blue eyes I'd ever seen came walking into my room. "Alice, I want to keep you overnight for observation just to make sure the fainting spells cease."

"Just overnight, right? I have a lot of school work to do." I told him.

"Don't worry about school work right now." Dr. Steele said in a fatherly tone. "Just relax and let me do my job. Aneurysms can be very, very dangerous if they burst, so you have to take your medication and stay on top of it."

By the time he had finished his sentence, in-walked Candy. "That's right! Don't worry, sir, I'm going to make sure she takes her medicine and keep up with her appointments too."

"Good. I'm glad you have a support system, Alice." Dr. Steele said, and then he excused himself to go see another patient. Within five minutes this white nurse walked in and greeted Candy. "Well, young lady, I have your medication to take." She handed me a small cup with two pills in it and a small cup of water to wash it down with. As the nurse was walking out, this X-ray tech walked in and told Candy and me that he will be coming to get me in ten minutes to take me down to get a CT scan done. "Okay." I said, and then I leaned back against the flat pillow with a sulk upon my face and closed my eyes because I felt so overwhelmed. Five minutes after the X-ray tech left, this young black woman came walking in with a badge that read: phlebotomist telling me that she had to draw some blood. I was about to blackout on someone because it was just too much. How the fuck was I supposed to get any sleep with all those people bothering me? Dr. Steele told me to relax but there was no way I could relax with everyone fuckin' with me.

Candy could see that I was getting annoyed but she tried to make light of things. "Alice, I'm going to grab me a cup of coffee. You what me to bring you anything?" It wasn't like we were home and she was going to the mall or anything. I was in the hospital for god sake! I looked at her like she was crazy. It was no time for her dry humor and I think she knew that by the look on my face. If only she knew, she was about to get cussed out ghetto-girl style.

***

Candy was standing by the coffee vending machine, when Dr. Steele approached her.

"Excuse me, ma'am. I didn't get a chance to catch your name, while you were in Alice's room." He said.

"Candy…Candy Brown."

"Ms. Brown, are you Alice's mother?"

"No, no. Um, unfortunately her mom was killed…"

"Oh. I'm so sorry to hear that."

Candy nodded her head.

"Well…"

Before Dr. Steele had a chance to finish his sentence Candy spoke. "I'm her guardian. Is there something wrong?"

"Well, I just wanted to talk to you about her aneurysm. It's like a ticking time bomb, so please, I can't stress this enough, please make sure she takes her medicine and visits the doctor regularly. If she ever gets really bad headaches like migraines rush her to the emergency room, immediately. This could be fatal if she is not attended to."

"I understand." Candy said while taking a sip of her black coffee.

Dr. Steele excused himself as Candy sat in the waiting

room area for a few minutes to digest everything that the doctor had said.

I'm her only family. Alice is like a daughter to me, Candy thought to herself. *What if something goes wrong? What if...*

There were so many thoughts rushing through Candy's mind. *She's graduating from college soon. She's such a responsible girl. Hopefully she'll land a great job at a prestigious accounting firm in the city. Alice had better take better care of herself.* Then Candy's thoughts were distracted as her eyes met this poster hanging on the wall of a mother and child embraced. It jogged her memory to remember to call her lawyer, Mr. Myles to check on Marlon's appeal date.

***

On my way to St. Joseph's Clinic on Market Street, for my follow-up appointment, my mind drifted thinking about Keith. Keith and I had been on about two or three dates, thus far, and I found myself getting a bit afraid. I was afraid because I was feeling too good and having too much fun. I felt guilty like I should've had the worst time and never wanted to see Keith again. But it was just the opposite. I always wanted to see him. Don't get me wrong, I loved Fat Boy with all of my heart, but I was beginning to feel lonely—lonely for a man's touch, smell, as well as his companionship. I got tired of watching Beverly, Tasha, Nikki and Casey talking about their booty-calls all the time. Talkin' about how much fun they had together. About their plans for the weekend while I stayed in my dorm room reading a friggin' Terry McMillan book trying to figure out how the hell could I get to *happy* too. Or, about them talking about their sex life. It really started to get to me because I could never join in the conversations with them. What...what was I supposed to say? "Oh, yeah, girl, I know what you mean...Fat Boy..." "Uh-huh, I go through the same thing with Fat Boy too..." "Just the other day Fat Boy and I had this big ass argument..." "Yeap. Yeap...Your man too...?" That was not my reality when it came to Fat Boy. I couldn't say *shit* because my man was behind bars. Yes, I had Fat Boy's back, but who had mines? No one. Up until I met Keith. And Keith was doing me doggy-style.

Yeah. I got tired of hearing, Dick this, Dick that... coming out of Beverly's mouth. Nearly every sentence had a "dick" in it. Bev was most definitely either obsessed with or deprived of *dick*.

I parked my car still deep in thought. I was fighting within myself. I was putting pressure on myself for living my life. C'mon, I only had one life. Wasn't it up to me to live it to its fullest. Isn't that what people say, "live life to the fullest" so what was the deal when it came to me following that advice, huh? I would never turn my back on Fat Boy. No. Not after all he's done for me. I guess, I did feel a sense of obligation to him. He saved my life. He was my prince in the 'hood and my knight in shining armor. He was the first young man to ever make love to me. I knew if Fat Boy wouldn't have gone to jail, I would have never stepped foot in Graceful's house, let alone Palace Playmates stripping myself bare.

The way I saw it I thought that Keith would just be company for me, someone to fill that void of loneliness, someone to cuddle up with. Never did I think that we would become sex partners. Never did I think that I would feel the way that I was feeling for him. I was supposed to be saving myself until Fat Boy came home. But things didn't happen exactly that way. Something definitely changed. I think, it was me. Yeah, I changed. And then my needs changed. My outlook on life changed too. I can't say that I understood right then, but something was working on me. What, I couldn't say. All I could say was that Keith was heavy on my mind. And the last time we had sex was on my mind too.

I found myself smiling from ear to ear like I was experiencing my first boy crush. *I could go for some dick tonight*, I thought to myself. Cut it out, girl, I told myself grinning from ear to ear.

As I entered the building to the clinic and was walking upstairs, this light-skinned, thin-framed woman with reddish-brown hair was coming down the steps. She had a pleasant look on her round face as she walked passed me, but before she stepped on the next step, she paused, and then she said, "Excuse me…" I figured she was talking to me because it was just she and I on the steps, so I turned around. Once I really took a good look at her, I noticed that she was the lady from St. Joseph's Regional Medical Center who did my CT scan. I had crossed paths with her on several different occasions, but I never could remember her name, so I never took the initiative to speak.

"Is Michele Banks your mom?" she asked me.

I nodded my head up and down.

"I knew it!" she said excitedly. "Oh, my name is Selena."

I cracked a smile.

Selena continued, "Your mom and I went to grammar and high school together. She sure did spit you out—such a pretty girl. I wanted to ask you the day I did your CT scan, but it totally slipped my mind after you had left."

I just listened to her talk. I didn't know exactly what to say. How to respond to her bringing up my mom, it was difficult to hear her say her name. I felt myself getting choked up. She must've noticed the pain in my eyes.

Her high-pitched voice reduced to melancholy and empathetic. "I'm sorry to hear about your mom."

"How did you know what happened to my mom?" I asked her. I answered my own question. She probably read about it in the newspaper, I said to myself.

"Your father Randy is my cousin," she explained.

"Wait a minute! You know my dad?"

She looked at me peculiarly. "Yes, your dad is my cousin. And he's been looking for you for quite a while now."

I swear I didn't believe her. I thought she was playing a cruel joke on me. I swore on everything that she was. He lives in Atlanta with his wife and children. He called me about a year ago and told me what happened to Michele. He asked me had I seen her before her murder. Then he told me about you and how he was having a difficult time locating you. Your father called every shelter, police department, and many other agencies looking for you."

I stood there in shock. I felt tears building up inside of me, but not one shed. Not one. I wanted to scream, but nothing would come roaring out. Nothing.

"I have his number. Do you want it?" she asked me.

I couldn't believe it. It seemed too easy—so surreal to me. I hadn't seen my father since my mom had kicked him out. That seemed like so many decades ago. What was I...six or seven years old back then? Wow.

"You know what I'ma do one better than that. I'ma call him right now. God is good," she said with a huge smile on her face as she pulled out her cell phone from her hunter-green smock front side pocket and called.

"Hello Randy, guess who's standing here in front of me."

"Who?" Randy asked in suspense.

"Alice."

There was silence on the other end of the phone. All that Selena could hear was Randy's heavy breathing. Then she gladly handed me her phone. I was disoriented, bewildered, angry, and bitter, there were so many mixed emotions flowing throughout my body. It took me a second or two to utter a word. It was like my mouth was paralyzed.

Finally, "Hello," came out, slowly and cautious. "Hello Randy." I said fearful that he wouldn't utter one word back to me.

"Hi Alice," he said like his stomach had dropped down to his feet. I could hear the concern in his tone. I can't tell you how good that made me feels—after all these years. We talked for about fifteen minutes. I didn't want to be inconsiderate on Selena's phone. I gave him my cell phone number and he gave me his cell and home phone number. We talked every day from that day going forward. Suddenly I didn't feel so alone.

Our relationship as father and daughter didn't bond right away. It took time, patience, trust, mostly trust because I didn't know if he'd come back into my life and then suddenly disappear again. I was mindful of that. Once someone hurts you, you learn from that experience.

I met my father's wife Leatravelle over the phone. We'd talk like we knew each other for years. I talked to his children too. To me I had an extended family.

After about three months, I found the nerve to confide in Randy about my life, but I failed to mention my indiscretions of stripping and hoeing. What girl wants their father to know about that? Well, I was no different. He was an estranged dad, but all in all, he was my dad, and he deserved a level of respect. I guess you could say I was too chicken to reveal news like that to him. I was embarrassed too. I did mention my enrollment in college. He said that he'd come to my graduation. I hoped he'd keep his word. I told him about Fat Boy and the situation surrounding the events that led to his incarceration. We seemed to hit it off well. We'd talk on the phone for hours upon hours, laughing and joking. God, I felt so at peace getting to finally know the man.

"Well, once you finish school, Alice, maybe you might wanna come and check out Atlanta."

"Maybe. I might wait until Fat Boy gets released. Maybe a change of scenery would be good for him too." I told him.

But deep down I figured Randy and I could possibly start off fresh in a new city like a new beginning.

"I always wanted to be in your life, Alice," he told me.

It was the way he said it that convinced me that maybe he was telling the truth. It was sincere, fatherly, and it brought tears to my eyes. Yeah. I felt his distant love for me. I felt it strong, hard, and meaningful.

"Is it true that you are twice mommy's age?" I asked him.

"Yes."

"Is it true that you used to get involved with illegal activities when you were young?" I asked him.

"Yes. But I loved Michele and when she got pregnant at seventeen years old, I panicked."

"She told me that you two had a lot of fun and were madly in love with each other." I told him.

He sighed, "Then she kicked me out of her home and out of your life."

There was a pause between the two of us.

"Alice, I'll never lose touch with you again, I promise." He said.

My dad started sending me money Western Union to help me out a little. I never asked, he always volunteered. It could've been because of guilt or maybe he just felt that I needed the extra cash. Who knows? I never pushed his generosity away. I didn't want to make him feel insignificant. I knew that it was difficult for the both of us, but here we were, making the best out of a bad situation.

I went to go visit Fat Boy two days after speaking to my dad. I told him that I wanted him to meet him. Fat Boy said that he couldn't wait to.

"Baby, maybe when I graduate you can meet him then. I can bring him here to the prison, if you don't mind."

"It ain't like I got too many options," Fat Boy said rather sarcastically. I didn't know for sure but I think Fat Boy was feeling a little uneasy about the whole situation, but like always he was a trouper. I guessed that's what I loved about him the most.

It was approaching graduation and everything was hectic. I was doing my best to stay calm, but final exams were keeping me stressed. Those exams were complicated, but I was ready. I had stayed up most of the nights to study. I knew that graduating on time was expected, mostly for me, and those who were a big part of my life—those who made an impact on me—those who had high expectations for me. I didn't want to disappoint anyone, including myself.

Randy was coming and I didn't want to let him down. We had a rapport with one another. We weren't best friends, but we were close in the last couple of months. When I talked to him over the phone he was so excited about seeing me. Candy was happy for me. And she was anxious to meet him too. I was really considering moving to Atlanta, and starting over. You know, new place, new people, and a new life. But I knew Fat Boy's appeal was coming up soon. I was feeling good about his conviction being overturned by the Governor. If not, it would be downgraded to a lesser charge like 2nd degree manslaughter or even a lower charge. Which in any case, it would be very short or he would have time to serve and be released. Either way it would be great news for the family.

I prayed everyday for the day for Fat Boy to come home.

***

Randy was loading his last few things in the car for his drive to New Jersey. He figured it would take him 15 hours the way he drives, and considering there was no heavy traffic.

After loading his olive-green Ford Expedition, he turned around and said goodbye to his kids and wife Leatravelle. Leatravelle joked with him about his fear of flying. "Baby, I can't believe you're going to drive. You,

Mr. Big Bad Randy is afraid to fly in an airplane." The kids giggled. She placed her hands on his hips, "You could be there in 2 ½ hours, if you'd fly."

Randy smiled gently. Leatravelle knew by the look on his face that she had triggered his last nerve, but he remained subtle in front of their kids. He nodded his head a couple of times, "And I could be dead in 2 ½ hours too if the plane crashes."

Leatravelle rolled her eyes, "There are more car accidents and less chances of having a plane crash, honey."

Randy basically nixed her comment off. "Yeah, yeah, yeah, you know who says that…people who fly. I have to be in control, in an airplane I'm not in control. When the plane goes down, it's over baby."

Leatravelle laughed out loud mostly at how melodramatic Randy could be. "Okay, you big baby. Have a safe drive."

They hugged and kissed; Randy kissed his kids, and pulled himself away, hopped in his SUV, and backed out of the driveway thinking about seeing Alice as a grown woman.

He turned on the radio to 104.1 FM, and as he turned onto 85 North heading to New Jersey, his mind drifted again. He was thinking about Michele, how they met, how much fun they used to have. He found himself getting misty-eyed thinking about how absent he had been in her life. And how he wished he kept some of the pictures they took together on a few occasions. Michele would always pull out a camera whenever he came around.

***

Saabs was walking down the tier. He stopped in front of this cell with a obese man sitting in his cell reading a fed magazine, "What's good, Pimpin'?" The man lifted up his head and said, "'Ey, Youngblood." If Saabs and the man who happened to be Graceful could've embraced each other with a brotherly hug they would have, but the cell bars separated the two.

Graceful was on the same side of the prison as Fat Boy. "You remember me?" Saabs asked him. Graceful took a hard good look. He nodded his head with a small gap in his mouth showing his gold-tooth. "Yeah, I did a coupla parties for you and your boys', right?"

"Yeah, that's right."

There was a moment of silence.

"Listen, I got some important words for you." Saabs told him.

"What's up, Youngblood?" Graceful narrow-eyed him.

"You know a nigga by the name of Fat Boy? Well, that's my cellmate. You used to pimp his woman. He blames you for turning her into a hoe. I have tried countless hours to change his mind, but he's hell-bent. Well, anyway, he got a shank and he's gonna try to stick you in the yard, so be careful, Pimpin'. I just wanted to give you a heads up, I ain't down with no player haters."

"Thanks, Youngblood, I owe you one," Graceful said, as Saabs walked away. "'Ey, Youngblood!" Graceful yelled, "Who was his bitch anyway?"

Saabs stopped in his tracks to listen, and then he answered. "Her name was Alice, but her stage name was Desire," Saabs replied.

Graceful remained silent and Saabs went on his way.

Ain't this a bitch, Graceful thought to himself. *She came to me...Egypt brought that bitch to me. Stupid ass nigga!* Graceful shook his head, annoyed, as he lifted himself up off of his mattress and slithered his chubby hand from underneath his mattress and pulled out his manmade metal knife and slipped it in his white long tube sock.

It was only minutes before the inmates would be forming a line and filing out to the yard. Fat Boy pushed his knife down the inseam of his boot. By this time, Saabs had retuned to their cell. He shook his head. "You really going to go through with this shit, man, ain't you." Saabs asked with a look of disappointment on his face. Fat Boy looked at Saabs, "I have to, I have to. What kind of man would I be if I didn't pay this fag pimp back?" He snapped.

"What about your appeal, Fat's?"

"Damn that, man."

"But...you're so close. They're sending you your decision any day now." Saabs tried to reason with him but Fat Boy's mind was made.

"FUCK THAT," Fat Boy roared back. "THIS SHIT HAS TO BE DONE!"

All the inmates were in the yard. Some were playing basketball, others playing handball. A lot of them were lifting weights. Graceful had his back toward the incoming inmates. He was facing a group of pimps, as they stood joking and talking game. Fat Boy was making his way through the crowd of muscle-bound bodies. He had his eyes glued to Graceful. His eyes were locked on his target and he was going in for the kill. Fat Boy was almost within striking distance. He reached down in his boot with his right hand and pulled out his knife. He drew his right arm back and brought it forward. One of Graceful's pimp buddies named Squatter, this black ugly dude who was facing him yelled, "LOOK OUT, GRACEFUL!!!" At that moment with lighting speed Graceful spun around and pushed his ten-inch metal knife right in Fat Boy's chest.

Fat Boy dropped his shank. He eyes looked like they were popping out of his head. He staggered backwards about two or three steps; there was only a little bloodstain around the wound. He put his arms out in front of him like he was asking for help. He then, hit the ground in one hard thump. Inmates stared moving quickly away in the other direction. The guards' setoff the sirens as they shot smoke bombs in the crowd, and then they rushed the yard and everyone was ordered to the ground. It was complete chaos in the prison's yard.

A bright light appeared, and Fat Boy found himself back at the DP station, where he first met Alice. He smiled, this warm endearing smile.

As the guards reached Fat Boy he was trying to speak, "tell her, tell her, I-I-I," the sound of blood gurgled in his throat. His eyes lay still open, although, the knife had pierced his heart.

***

"Okay, Randy. I mean Daddy. Sorry, I'm still getting use to all of this." I told him over the phone.

"Baby," Randy said in a gentle tone, "You can call me whatever you want to."

They both laughed which broke the ice.

"So how much longer before you get here, Dad?" I asked him.

Randy glanced at his clock. "Oh, probably about four more hours, I think. As long as I don't run into anymore traffic. What time is the graduation?"

"It's at 10:00 a.m., this morning. You remember my dorm room number, right?"

"Yes, baby, I got everything written down. I should be there about 8:00 a.m., honey."

"Okay, drive safely. I can't wait to see you!"

"All right, see you in a little while. I love you, Alice."

Just hearing him say those words made me feel so good inside. "I love you, too. Oh, Dad, I have a picture I want to show you when you get here. I had it ever since I was a little girl. I kept it safe and near me."

"Okay, baby, I'll see you soon. Bye."

"Bye."

I decided to take a shower that way I would have more time to spend with my dad once he arrived. My roommate had gone home and was coming to the graduation in the morning with her parents. I walked over to my bed and laid my cap and gown across the bed. I slithered my fingers in and underneath my mattress and pulled out the picture wrapped in plastic wrap and I laid it on top of my gown. I stood there and just gazed at it for what seemed like a lifetime. I finally made it to graduation day. I was so happy.

I walked into the bathroom and turned the nozzle to the shower on. I undressed out of my hot pink boy shorts and lime-green T-shirt and stepped inside the shower, and adjusted the water to lukewarm.

***

On the first floor, the water leaked down from the ceiling, this student called security to report the leak. After several calls the janitor searched each dorm to find out where the leak was coming from. "I have to check upstairs," the blonde haired man told security.

Randy was pulling up in the campus parking lot. He tried calling Alice numerous times in the last hour, but she never picked up. He assumed she might've dozed off to sleep. With one small suitcase in his hands, Randy headed toward Alice's dorm room.

The janitor repeatedly knocked on Alice's door. He heard what sounded like the radio or TV on, but no one answered, so he asked security to come up with the master key. The security guard and Randy arrived at Alice's door simultaneously. "Excuse me, is something wrong?" Randy asked with a concerned look on his face. The security guard asked, "Who are you?" Randy responded, "I'm

Alice Banks, father. This is my daughter's dorm room."

"Oh, okay," the security guard, said, "we have a leak and it might be coming from her room. We need to check it but no one is answering so I had to bring the key up to Mike, our janitor."

The security guard stuck several keys in the door before it had opened. When the security guard, the janitor, and Randy stepped foot in, they didn't say anything. They all heard the water running from the bathroom. The bathroom light was on. The door was ajar. Randy knocked on the door and called out Alice's name.

Knock, "Alice, Alice," Knock, knock. He repeated his steps. But there was still no answer. "Alice, honey is you in there?" Still, there was no answer.

At that moment, they noticed the water flowing from underneath the door. Randy pushed the door open and there was Alice lying unconscious dangling over the bathtub. Her arms seemed lifeless as her hair hid her face. She hung there like a rag doll. Randy raced over to her, kneeled down beside her. He screamed to the men to call 911! He carefully pulled Alice out of the bathtub and laid a towel over her naked body. He tried to perform CPR, but Alice's body was limp. He cradled her in his arms like a newborn baby.

"Alice, Alice, it's me, Daddy. Please wake up! Please wake up…" he pleaded with tears engulfed in his eyes. "Get some help, somebody do something…this is my little girl," with body-jerking tears he hovered over her and hugged her so tightly and squeezed her so close to his heart.

Randy thought he saw her eyes flicker open and then slowly closed again. The voice seemed like it was far away, but it was close and personal. As Alice was slipping into the distance of her mind, she managed to crack a smile as a flash of Fat Boy's face briefly appeared.

As darkness came over her, Alice saw the faces of Michele, Steve, Mr. and Mrs. Dempsey and Fred—it was all a reminder of a life she *once* lived. Vaguely she heard this manly voice again, and then it faded in the distance. She felt a touch that was as light as a feather brush against her face. Relief and joy came over her as she opened her eyes seeing her father finally there. At last she knew he *loved* her, but her secret would stay secured within herself. Randy would never know: *How She Became A HOE.*

Epilogue

Randy stood looking at Alice's cap and gown lying neatly across her bed. Tears rolled down his cheeks like waterfalls. He couldn't accept the tragedy that was upon him. As he stood there he noticed a picture wrapped in clear plastic wrap next to his right foot. It must've fallen off the bed. He bent down and picked it up, while wiping the tears with his left backhand. As he unfolded the plastic wrap his body shivered, as a warm smile of love tried to triumph through all the pain. Randy gazed at the picture of Michele, Alice, and him; he nodded his head in reminiscence of the day the picture was taken a long time ago.

***

On the other side of town, the phone rang. Candy answered it.

"Hello."

"Candy!" The voice on the other end said. It was her lawyer Mr. Myles. "CANDY, THE CONVICTION IS OVERTURNED! THE CONVICTION HAS BEEN OVERTURNED! I JUST GOT THE PHONE CALL! Your son is coming home! He's coming home!"

Candy screamed at the top of her lungs so full of joy. She began jumping up and down. She could not compose herself as she called for her daughter, "Jada, Jada, Marlon's coming home!" Tears burst from Candy's eyes. Her heart was racing at rapid speed. She was so overcome with joy. Finally, her boy was coming home. Jada ran into the living room hollering and jumping up and down with her short arms swinging in the air screaming with big teardrops flowing down her small face. She missed her big brother so much. And now he was finally coming home.

THE END

FEMALE FRIENDS
(WHO HAVE GIVEN ME THEIR SUPPORT AND HONEST
OPINION ABOUT MY WORK)

CYNTHIA ANDERSON-DARBY
CHERRY DEJESUS
RACHEAL MCNEIL
TAWANA SMITH
CHERYL WILLIAMS
COURTNEY STEEDE
SHANTIA CLYBURN
DEBBIE FRYE
STACEY & TARA
SIMIKA JACKSON
KIM WILLIAMS
SHEEMA NEWAN
KIM JONES
PATRICA HAMRICK-ANDERSON
LEATRAVELLE FLEMING
LATOYA BRUNSON
LENA HALL
DENA RODGERS
CHERYL LYNN-HODGES
DONNA MCFARLAND
MI BESOS RODRIGUEZ

I couldn't possibly name everyone who gave me
congrats on my 1st and 2nd book, but I would like to say,
"Thank you, all."

Paterson Pimp

SHOUTOUT TO PATERSON BROTHERS LOCKDOWN

DONALD WRIGHT
MONTE "FATHER FIZZ" WADE (Cousin)
GARY "MUTA" NERO
GREGORY "DON JUAN" SHANNON
KEITH "KAHEEM" HILL (17TH AVE)
NATHAN "NASHON" JONES (17TH AVE)
JIMMY "JUSTICE" JOSEY (17TH AVE)
FRANK "BOOBIE" CULBREATH
MYRON "BELOVE" WIBERLY (17TH AVE)
MICHAEL RITTER
ANTHONY HUSKY
FREDERICK STONE
WILLIAM "COOLSHAWN" SERMAN (17TH AVE)
DOUGLAS "I-POWER" MASON (17TH AVE)
"AZ" (17TH AVE)
"CHARLIE" (17TH AVE)
BIG NICK (17TH AVE)
TAMORIE HILL (17TH AVE)
DASHAWN MITCHELL

And to all the Brothers and Sistas Lockdown,

Keep Ya Head Up!

HOES

(WHERE YA'LL AT?)

Lookin' for Hoes who don't mind sharing how they got into the game. Need honest hoes that are able to tell their stories in explicit and truthful detail. Lookin' for Hoes that can articulate from the beginning to the end of how their hoe-lifestyle began. Tell of who got you into it and why. Are you still hoein' till this day and why haven't you sought out for professional help? Are there any benefits to being a hoe? What does hoein' mean to you? Is it painful or pleasurable? Why haven't you stopped? Or can you stop? And if you can't stop what's holdin' you down? Are you addicted, trapped, confused, or do you simply enjoy gettin' your pussy popped by untrusting, grimy niggas?

If you feel that you are one of many who are not afraid to share your experience, contact Jashon763@aol.com and tell me your story. Nah. This is not a paying gig so don't expect any money from me. This is just a compilation of stories for my next book about how females become hoes. There is no word-count for this project.

***ONLY SERIOUS HOES NEED TO REPLY. My time is valuable.

The Paterson Pimp a.k.a Jashon
J&M Production Publishing
52 Washington Street,
P.O. Box 20, Paterson, NJ 07501

THANK YOU FOR READING,

HOW SHE BECAME A HOE

VISIT THE SITE TO LEARN MORE
ABOUT
THE PATERSON PIMP

www.ThePatersonPimp.com

E-MAIL: **ThePatersonPimp@aol.com**
FACEBOOK: **Randy "Jashon" Jackson**

Order Form

Photocopies of this form will be accepted for ordering.

Book Title:	Price:	Copies:	Total:
My Soul Is Still Pimpin	$12.95	_____	_____
The Paterson Pimp	$14.95	_____	_____
How She Became A Hoe	$14.95	_____	_____
Shipping & Handling			
Per Book	$ 4.95	_____	_____
For Inmates	$ 0.00		$0.00
		Total	_____

NOTE: **FREE S&H** for all inmates who are currently incarcerated.

Accepted Forms of Payment: Check, Money Order, Online Payments via check or credit card through Paypal. If you are ordering for an inmate, please be sure to include their inmate number in the shipping address.

Shipping:

Name: _____ Inmate #: _____

Address: _____

City: _____ State: _____ Zip: _____

Send All Payments To:
J& M Production/Publishing
52 Washington Street, P.O. Box 20
Paterson, New Jersey 07501

Buy Online: www.The PatersonPimp.com